INTO DEATH SHORT STORY
COLLECTION

SAILING WITH
Mystery

M. A. LEE

Sailing with Mystery

"Amber Dreams" "Purple Poison" "Black Heart"

"Silver Web" "Red Mask"

Copyright © 2023 Emily Dunn & Writers Ink Books

First Published in the United States of America

Cover and Title Page by Deranged Doctor Design

www.writersinkbooks.com

WRITERS INK BOOKS

Contents

Amber Dreams

1

Isabella propped her sketch to dry against the wall at the back of her bunk. The smooth sailing of the day reassured her that it wouldn't topple over.

Propping the sketch on the bunk wasn't ideal, but in her few days aboard the passenger ship *Nomadic*, she hadn't discovered a better place in the third-class berth. She shared the tight quarters with three other young ladies. Hettie Rufford's climb to the top bunk still disconcerted her, but chattering with new friends was an unexpected benefit.

Luck had flown with her when she finished her portrait for the dowager Lady Malvaise much earlier than anticipated. The booking office had recorded a cancellation the morning that she arrived to ask about an earlier berth. She sent blessings to whoever had cancelled their reservation, for she would join Madoc a month earlier than originally planned. A voyage of forty days with an additional five days ashore in Port Said, waiting to transfer to a ship that plied the Indian Ocean, would be no great matter.

She slipped into her strappy heels then fluffed the gathered skirt of her black frock before stepping to the mirror mounted above the tiny washstand.

"As lovely as that frock is," Nedda Cortland shared, swinging a slippered foot as she lounged on the lower bunk, "you'll need something more, Isabella. You will certainly need more for a stroll on the deck under the moonlight." She turned another page in the fashion magazine she'd confiscated from the first-class Reading Room.

Isabella gave an inelegant snort. "No moonlit strolls for me, but I will take my India shawl." She retrieved the brightly-colored wrap from her bunk and shook it loose from its folds. "Are you certain that you'll be fine here?" *Fine alone*, she meant, for on the past evenings they'd dined together, braving the crowded second-class dining room to enjoy a bland meal more filling than tasty.

The secretary lifted her dark gaze from the glossy pages. "The steward will bring a tray, and I intend to enjoy a few hours alone. Not even Hettie or Caro should disturb me," she added, naming their roommates. "Go on. You will be late, which will not be an auspicious beginning to an evening with Mr. Ingram. You have his invitation? You will need it to enter the first-class dining room."

She waved her silver-beaded purse. "I have it here. You are certain, Nedda?"

The secretary rolled her eyes then straightened from her lounge on the lower bunk. She tugged the silky flamboyant wrap onto her shoulder. "Stop havering over this opportunity to enjoy first-class."

Isabella laughed and went.

The trek from third-class sent her along narrow passageways and up three flights of stairs to reach the Promenade Deck, above the main deck. The *Nomadic* was a larger ship in the British-Asia Oceanic Navigation line. With a single-funnel and four masts, it was considered one of the premier ships traveling from Britain to the Mediterranean.

BAON offered four types of accommodation to passengers. Gold Star denoted first-class passengers with staterooms on the promenade deck and the first deck. Silver and Bronze Star meant second- and third-class passengers. The majority of those traveling, these passengers were housed in the second two lower decks. The Red Star fourth-class, the smallest contingent aboard, were deeper into the ship, rarely emerging into areas shared by the other passengers.

British-Asia Oceanic prided itself on its treatment of all passengers, but Red Star lacked any amenities, including a dining room. They had only a canteen and had to eat in their cramped, dormitory-style berths.

Madoc had warned Isabella not to take a fourth-class berth. She had saved money with a third-class berth, considering what was acceptable for the servants of first-class passengers would be acceptable for her. Thus, she met Nedda Cortland, secretary to the wealthy financier Hyatt Ingram, and two personal maids, Hettie Rufford and Caro Marten. She rarely saw Hettie and Caro, but she and Nedda had formed an alliance.

After a working lunch with her employer, Nedda had spotted Isabella on deck with her watercolors. The secretary had guided Mr. Ingram to meet her new friend. This evening's invitation to the first-class dining room was the result. That encounter, Isabella suspected, was a carefully planned subterfuge to win time away from a demanding employer.

She didn't begrudge Nedda seizing a chance for solitude. Like a little city on the ocean waves, the *Nomadic* was crowded, with few places for a solitary retreat. Of the four in their shared berth, only Isabella was not at someone else's beck-and-call. While she relished deciding how to spend her free hours, she sympathized with her three roommates, working as hard aboard as they would on land.

In the first-class dining room, hundreds of candles softened the ship's harsh light. Floral arrangements graced the tables. China and crystal and silver sparkled on crisp white linens.

Isabella followed the *maître d'* to a prominent table already half-filled. A *sommelier* listened to Mr. Ingram's instructions. She assumed the other two at the table were his son and grandson, mentioned this afternoon. The men rose as the steward drew out a chair on the table's long side, one of four.

"Charming, charming," the financier murmured. Approaching his seventies, he still looked hale, eyes clear and bearing upright. "Mrs. Tarrant, my son Sheridan, my grandson Colfax. Mrs. Madoc Tarrant, the artist."

Sheridan Ingram had his father's long face and neat appearance, but pouches beneath his eyes and forming jowls hinted at dissipation. He gave a hearty pleasantry which Isabella returned. The grandson barely lifted his eyes from table. Colfax Ingram had a couple of inches on his father. The pads in his jacket couldn't hide his narrow shoulders.

The men started to sit only to stand again as others reached the table. Leading the way was an elderly woman in black *crepe de chine* with a floral georgette swath at the neckline and over the skirt of her gown. With her silver hair piled high, sparkling with diamante pins, she looked to have more than a decade on Hyatt Ingram.

Following her and quick to draw out her chair as hostess was a man with a thin mustache and a military bearing. Isabella couldn't place his age, somewhere in his thirties.

Coming last was a fashionable couple of Sheridan Ingram's age, Mr. and Mrs. Neal Gallagher. He wore a cerise tie and matching pocket square with his white dinner jacket. Mrs. Gallagher's gown, a long sheath with a flared skirt, matched her husband's flash of cherry-pink.

Two chairs still remained empty. As Isabella exchanged greetings with the newcomers, she wondered who had yet to appear.

Their hostess was Lady Serilda Peverell. Isabella knew the name, for her roommate Hettie Rufford was the woman's maid. The military man, Colonel Emerson Werthy, took the chair on Isabella's right. Mr. and Mrs. Neal Gallagher separated, the man to Mr. Ingram's left and his wife to Lady Peverell's right. At first glance Isabella had thought him older than his wife, but as he spoke across table to Sheridan Ingram, ignoring the sulky grandson, she adjusted that age downward, deeming them nearer in age to Col. Werthy than her own of 25.

As the stewards served a chilled cocktail, two women arrived to take the last seats at table. The one in a flurry of crocheted shawl and fly-away curls with threads of grey was Miss Arabella Swandon. She tittered about her tardiness and difficulties with finding the table and gave a "hallo" to everyone, repeated to Colfax beside her until he deigned to look up and nod. From that Isabella guessed that only the Ingrams and Lady Peverell always had this table. The others shifted around at will for each dinner.

The svelte woman strolled behind Miss Swandon. She waited for her chair to be withdrawn, done with alacrity by Col. Werthy. Over a simple chemise of aubergine she wore a *haut couture* gown with beaded embellishments on the elaborate embroidery. She introduced herself as Mrs. Phoebe Drake. Isabella expected the able colonel would ignore her to attend to Mrs. Drake, but he surprised her. He gave them both equal attention as the courses progressed through a consommé, baked cod in butter, then a ragout of oxtail.

The entrée was an excellent beef *tournado*. She enjoyed it even more when she recalled last night's curried chicken and rice, preceded by a rice soup and followed by rice pudding. With a bite in her mouth, though, the conversation turned to her. She should have expected it. Lady Peverell had speared the others at table, course by course. The Gallaghers were queried during the cocktail and soup, Mrs. Drake during the fish, and Miss Swandon during the ragout.

She swallowed her bite of beef as Mr. Ingram explained how she came to join their table.

"An artist?" Lady Peverell frowned, a minatory gaze looking for a flaw in Isabella's appearance. "What brings you aboard ship?"

She gave a silent thanks to her friend Flick Sherbourne for the paisley shawl and to her sister-in-law Cecilia for the Lanvin-style frock, simple elegance in black satin woven to resemble silk. The elderly woman's eagle eyes had likely spotted the inexpensive fabric. Isabella lifted her chin and gave a smile that belied her jitters. "I sail to join my husband in India."

"A planter?" Sheridan Ingram leaned forward to look uptable. "With which company?"

"He's not a planter. He's with Tredennit Builders."

Col. Werthy hmphed. "Road building," he informed the others. "A contract in Australia, isn't it?"

Her view of the colonel warmed. "It is, but I know very little. Madoc has only been employed with Tredennit since the New Year."

"Tarrant. Tarrant." Neal Gallagher tapped his knife on his plate. "I've heard that name. Read it. In the newspapers."

Eyes swiveled her way. She swallowed air this time. Only careful maneuvering would keep the topic away from salacious gossip about murders, the arrests of Frederick Petrie and Nigel Arkwright, and Cecilia Arkwright's subsequent marriage to Madoc's brother Gawen. "My brother-in-law is a renown archaeologist. Professor Gawen Tarrant at St. George's University. He is publishing a series of articles about his archaeological dig on the island of Crete. I did the drawings with the articles."

"Pen and ink?" the colonel asked. "And watercolors. I saw you working this afternoon. Do you use any other medium?"

Before she could answer, Mrs. Gallagher asked, "Do we dock at Crete? It would be fascinating to visit an actual archaeological dig. We would touch history."

"I've seen one of your paintings," Lady Peverell declared. "An oil of young Edward Malvaise."

"Yes, my lady, I completed that portrait in the last month. To have seen it, you must be well acquainted with the dowager Lady Malvaise? It hangs in her private suite at the family estate."

"She was most pleased with your work, Mrs. Tarrant. She advised all of us to commission you before you sailed for the South Seas."

"I escaped all commissions, my lady. I had to finish my work for Prof. Tarrant and a few pen-and-inks for Tony Carstairs. He offers my work in his gallery."

"Is it a nice portrait of the Malvaise boy?" Miss Swandon asked. "He's the only one still alive after the war, isn't he?"

The dowager Peverell ignored the interruption. "She said you were not the usual artist."

A raised voice at a nearby table stopped any reply. "You do not have my permission to write to him," a man declared.

The comment drew the eyes of all who had heard, passengers and stewards alike. Colfax Ingram turned in his seat while Isabella's side of the table watched without displaying such rude interest.

The couple were smartly dressed. The young woman wore a stylish embroidered peacock gown. A glittering tie pin detracted from the understated elegance of the man's crisp suit. As he berated her about her role as a Stropeford bride, Isabella didn't envy them at all.

The young woman had lowered her gaze to her plate. Her murmured response did not reach their table. Nor did it placate her companion.

He withdrew white rectangles from an inner pocket and cast them down. One fluttered open to land on the daisy-filled posy. Then he drew out an envelope and waved it under his wife's nose. "What do you have to say for yourself?"

At the snap in his voice, Isabella flinched. She wanted to look away, yet her gaze was captured by the train wreck. The Gallaghers and Miss Swandon had twisted around, copying Colfax's obvious staring.

The bride reached for the envelope only to have the man snatch it back. "You dare write to him after—." He lowered his voice, hiding the words although not his harsh tone.

Col. Werthy started from his seat. Mrs. Drake put a hand on his arm.

Hyatt Ingram loudly cleared his throat. "Steward!"

The man looked up then. When he saw the censure over this public drama coming multiple tables, he flushed red. His chair scraped the floor as he stood. He tossed the envelope onto the table before he strode out.

In a flurry of jerky actions, the young woman hastened after him.

The whole room watched. When the doors closed, talk resumed, loud and clattery in the first moments before settling down as people overcame amazement.

"We shall see what we shall see," Lady Peverell intoned.

The steward had arrived. "More wine," the elder Ingram ordered.

The man lifted a hand, and a younger steward appeared with a new bottle. He uncorked it and poured a mouthful, which he offered to Mr. Ingram for approval. Everyone watched him taste the wine. He commented to Mr. Gallagher and the colonel about the vintage.

The first steward moved away as the younger one began filling goblets with the new wine.

"A cabernet," Mr. Ingram informed them. "You will enjoy it with the beef."

"Oh my!" Miss Swandon fanned herself. "I usually have only one glass at dinner."

The financier smiled like a benevolent uncle bestowing a treat. "Tonight you will have two."

Lady Peverell lifted a finger, and the first steward bent to listen to her. Then he stepped to the abandoned table. His body blocked his action, but when he returned, he handed the folded notes and the letter to the elderly lady. She slipped them into her beaded purse. Her gaze then speared Isabella. "Mrs. Tarrant, you and I shall have a talk in the morning. At 11 o'clock in my stateroom."

That sounded ominous. Isabella could give only one answer. "Of course, Lady Peverell."

2

Clouds promised rain. Waves washed high against the ship, promising choppy seas. Passengers determined to complete a promenade crowded the decks.

Isabella caught snippets about cricket test matches, politics, new inventions, and the latest fashions, but she scarcely heeded what she heard. Her eyes busily spotted the difference in accommodations as she traveled from Bronze Star passageways to Silver Star and then Gold Star.

The first-class passageways were wide and carpeted. Gilt mirrors replaced the cheap paintings of the second-class walls, and glass chandeliers rather than wall sconces lit the way for the privileged. Two stewards stopped her in first class, ostensibly to offer directions along the corridors they attended. The second escorted her to Lady Peverell's stateroom on the upper deck, even knocking on the door and ensuring Isabella was admitted before returning to his post.

Hettie Rufford opened the door. By no word or sign did the maid reveal that she knew Isabella. She merely stepped back for Isabella to pass then disappeared into a narrow chamber off to the side.

Wearing a *plissé* nightrobe with lace ruffles adorning the neck and wrists and hem, Lady Peverell sat enthroned on a reproduction Louis XIVth chair facing the door. Her silver hair was still undressed, tied with a silky ribbon and trailing across her shoulder.

The surprising addition to this conversation was the young woman of last evening's event. She had taken the low settee at the foot of a curtained bed. Her fashionable navy sailor suit emphasized the darkness under her eyes.

Lady Peverell pointed to the other Louis XIVth chair. "You are prompt,

Mrs. Tarrant, which I appreciate. Rufford." She didn't lift her voice, but the maid quickly appeared. "Absent yourself for a half-hour. I think our interview will last no longer than that. I shall dress then."

The maid curtsied then slipped away, closing the stateroom door with the barest snick.

Lady Peverell fixed her gaze on the young woman, who visibly quelled.

Isabella took pity on her. "I do not believe we've been introduced. I am Isabella Tarrant, an artist. Lady Peverell is a new acquaintance. We have the dowager Lady Malvaise in common." When the young woman merely stared at her twisting fingers, she prompted, "I thought your gown last evening was lovely. Is that a new design from the Maison Myrbor?"

The opening worked. "It's a Worth original, part of my trousseau." She plucked at the pleated hem of her walking skirt. "This is part of my trousseau. Everything I have is part of my trousseau."

So, the wedding was recent, and the husband's dictatorial ways were likely a shock. Isabella still couldn't divine the reason that Lady Peverell wanted them to meet.

"Oh," the young woman said, "I forgot. You do not know my name or my circumstances or anything." Her voice faded on the last word.

The dowager's gaze had fixed on the young woman. "Our time is passing, Gemma."

She flinched. Her gaze darted around, avoiding them to fix upon an ornate gilded escritoire. "You'll think I'm a foolish flit."

"No, of course—."

"He thinks I am. Perhaps I am. I never should have agreed—." Her gaze switched to Isabella. Dam broken, the words gushed out. "I wouldn't have, but the terms were so beneficial. Papa will keep his horses and Mummy will have her teas and soirées and Augie will continue at Oxford. Although he doesn't really suit Oxford. He wants to be in London. I don't think he'll make a scholar. But I agreed, and I thought it wouldn't matter. I could forget him and go on with my life. Close my eyes and think of England, that's what Mummy said. But I can't forget him. I didn't know how much I would think of him. We shouldn't have met, those times before the ceremony, but we did, and after, too, in the six weeks before we sailed, and that's when it happened, and I don't regret that it happened. I don't regret it at all. I have good memories now. *He* shouldn't care. *He* has what he wants, a pretty bride to spend fripperies on. I should have what I want. But here I am, stuck with him. That room is so small, and there's no escape, and it will go on for weeks. For weeks! And now he's discovered, not everything, of course, but enough. I never expected him to be jealous. Fancy that. He's jealous."

The spate of words ended. She looked at Lady Peverell while Isabella floundered, trying to make sense of what she'd heard.

"Men are territorial, my dear."

"Yes, my lady, I know that now. It's still a surprise. Are you married?" she asked Isabella. "Did your husband die in the war?"

"I am traveling to India to join him. We married at the end of January."

"You're newly wed, too. Is he territorial? Is he jealous?"

"I haven't encountered that in him, no."

She sank against the settee. "My bad luck, to be saddled with a man who is jealous."

"You married two months ago?" she hazarded a guess.

"Seven weeks and five days. Seven weeks and five days as Lady Stropeford. No one calls me by my own name anymore. Lady Peverell does. I just realized! No one calls you by your own name, do they, my lady?"

"I would call you by your name," Isabella offered, "if you would share it with me."

"Oh, I am foolish! I'm Gemma. Gemma Farraday. Only now I'm Lady Stropeford, wife of Lord Douglas Stropeford."

"And the man you can't forget?"

"Ramsey Kemp."

"I suppose it's more than letters?"

Gemma's mouth dropped open. Lady Peverell gave a decisive nod. "I knew you were the one we needed. Gemma's diary is missing. She discovered it gone from her vanity case yesterday morning. You saw her husband confront her with a letter and two folded pages, which were torn from the diary. This morning, on her breakfast tray, was another page from the diary." She produced the folded papers that the steward had retrieved for her last evening. "He's taken her diary, very likely to hold as evidence should he ever wish to dissolve the marriage."

"All my hopes and dreams are in that diary. Two years. My foolish whimsies. My sorrows and unhappiness."

"How did you discover that he had taken your diary?"

"Mrs. Tarrant, did I not say that her husband confronted her with two of the pages and this letter at dinner last evening?"

"But Lady Peverell, Gemma didn't pick up those pages. Nor did she take the letter. The steward handed all three to you."

The dowager leaned back. Her gaze drifted back as she recalled the evening, then she gave a curt nod. "You are correct. Gemma, how did you know?"

"I discovered the diary missing yesterday morning. I always write in the morning while I have my tea. It wasn't in my vanity case, where I keep it. And he had those pages. He had to have taken it."

"What does the diary look like? Is it like any book? Is there a particular color?"

"It is a book. The cover is orange."

"You didn't see it anywhere in your stateroom?"

"I looked in all the drawers and in all his things, his shaving kit and briefcase and everything! It's nowhere in the room. My maid also looked. She didn't find it either."

"Your maid is familiar with where you keep it?"

"She hands it to me after she brings my tea tray."

"She removes the diary from the vanity case?"

"Of course."

Isabella nodded as she imagined the scene: Gemma sipping her tea, waiting for the diary to come to her hand. The maid searching the vanity case then the dressing table, thinking that it must have been mislaid the morning before. Both women searching the room, first the drawers and closet assigned to them, then the ones assigned to Lord Stropeford, and then into his closed luggage still stored in the room.

"There was another page on my tray yesterday morning."

"What?" She jerked back to attention. "Yesterday morning? When you realized the diary was missing?"

"The page was tucked under my teacup. He had to have added it to my tray. He must have!"

No, that didn't make sense. If Stropeford planned to confront his young wife at dinner, why would he add a page to her tea tray in the morning? "Did he say anything to you?"

"Only what you heard."

"And two diary pages came with your morning tea, yesterday and today?" she confirmed, her mind quickly re-sorting all of her assumptions.

"Of course."

"What are you thinking, Mrs. Tarrant?"

"That Lord Stropeford has nothing to do with the missing diary."

"That's not possible. He had to have taken it. Who else would?"

"What did the note say? What did last evening's notes say?"

Gemma reached into her slim purse and withdrew a folded paper. Lady Peverell handed over the notes she had taken last evening.

Isabella quickly scanned the four pages. A rounded school-girl hand covered both sides of the cream-colored paper. The torn edges revealed the diary's handsewn binding. She caught "marvelous party", "danced to dawn", "eager to see him again" and "tea with Mummy", chatter about a shopping trip. One page ended with the word "kiss"; the next page, still in the diary, obviously contained incriminating information.

The pages had no names, no dates or locations, just the effusive wishes for something else, rambling dissatisfaction with her new husband, a hope that she would soon return to London where she could be free. That one was dated to a few days before, the morning after they left port in Southhampton.

Not one page gave enough evidence for Lord Stropeford to launch divorce proceedings against his bride.

If that was the purpose for stealing the diary.

What other purpose could there be? Why remove pages from the diary if they were not incriminating?

"Is this what you usually write in the diary?"

Gemma clutched her hands together. Once more they began twisting. "I did write some things, in the weeks before we sailed, that I wouldn't want anyone to read."

Isabella handed the notes back. "You should keep these. How did your husband come by that letter?"

"He must have taken it from my maid. I gave it to Tamman to give to Rufford to mail for me."

That convoluted plan had drawn attention to Gemma's desire to hide the letter from her husband. Isabella wanted to roll her eyes, but she didn't. "Could the valet have taken your diary? Did he know where it was kept?"

"I don't know. Henredon has seen me writing in it."

"The valet's name is Henredon? Where would I find him this afternoon?"

"I couldn't say."

Lady Peverell interrupted Isabella's questions. "You think the valet has the diary? Why would he take it?"

"Loyalty to his master. Or—Gemma, you've not received any demands for money?"

"I have no money. Stropeford pays for everything."

"Do you not receive an allowance?"

"I do, but I do not need access to it while we're aboard."

"Blackmail?" the dowager asked.

"Perhaps," Isabella slowly agreed, her mind spinning scenarios. "Or loyalty, as I said. Only three people had easy access to the diary."

"Three? Who else besides Stropeford or his valet?"

"The maid."

"Tamman? Certainly not," Gemma declared. "She is loyal to me. She's been with me since before my marriage."

Isabella didn't point out that the pages provided to Lord Stropeford had had nothing incriminating on them. "Who else has access to your stateroom?"

"Well, the stewards, the maids who come in to clean, the man who carried in my trunk from cargo. He had to wait several minutes, you see, before Tamman told him to return the trunk to baggage. Tamman had packed my best gown in it, thinking I wouldn't need it until we reached Port Said. Then we were invited to dine with Captain Pitney, and I had to have that gown."

"Do you keep your vanity case locked?"

"It's supposed to be, but we were at sixes and sevens that afternoon, in such a rush. We had to wait all morning for the trunk. Tamman could have left it unlocked. He could have spotted it."

Lady Stropeford rambled on, but Isabella had already rejected the sailor working in cargo. He wouldn't have known the diary contained anything important.

The torn-out pages—. She mused over those. Nothing incriminating except for complaints about Lord Stropeford. As a source for evidence in a divorce, they were weak—unless they were an opening volley in Lord Stropeford's campaign to undermine his wife. They were equally weak as a source for blackmail … unless they were a threat. The first page, on the breakfast tray, pointed out that the diary was missing. The second pages, given to Lord Stropeford, proved how easily the husband would learn of his wife's perfidy. This morning's note confirmed that threat.

Lady Peverell leaned forward. "You don't think Stropeford has anything to do with the diary?"

"He might. If he hasn't had a chance to read the diary completely, he might have torn out pages at random. Has he mentioned divorce?"

Gemma shook her head. "Not a word, not until last evening, and you heard what he said."

And none of that was about divorce.

"Stropeford can make of it what he will, but none of this is evidence for divorce. Stropeford has told me that he does not want a divorce. Gemma herself does not want a divorce," the dowager said with certainty.

The young woman nodded vehemently. "We would have to return the settlements. No horses for Papa. No salons and weeks in London for Mummy. Augie might have to take a position." She whispered the last, as if a job was a high crime.

Isabella couldn't think of a good response to that. She aimed for the heart of the problem. "Gemma, you have my sympathies, of course, you do, but I am not certain what you expect my involvement to be. Lady Peverell, what would you have me do?"

"Recover the diary. It's not in their stateroom. Gemma has searched, as has her maid and my Rufford. Stropeford has hidden it. I wish you to find it."

"Perhaps it's in the ship's safe?"

"He wouldn't risk the purser or his staff reading the diary. He has no trusted acquaintances aboard ship."

Isabella blinked, thinking of the size of the ship, the many places that the diary might be hidden. These two women had fastened upon Lord Stropeford as the culprit, ignoring all of Isabella's doubts. She tried a different solution, one that would be impossible to check. "Perhaps Lord Stropeford wrapped it as a package and left it in the mailroom to ship home."

Lady Peverell looked pleased at that idea. "We did not think of that, not at all. You are the person to help us. I knew it. You can ask about a package without word being sent to Stropeford."

"My lady—."

The older woman continued over the interruption. "Lady Malvaise told me that you solved Tommy Gresham's murder. And there was a murder on the archaeological dig where you met your husband. You can solve this little mystery, I am certain."

"My lady, I am flattered by your faith in me, but I had nothing to do with solving those murders."

"Nonsense. Lady Malvaise told me *everything*."

"You are wonderful," Gemma gushed. "I was in such dumps. You'll be a good friend to me. I know it. I have such relief!"

A knock came on the door. Gemma broke off as the door opened, and the maid slipped inside. "Lord Stropeford is coming, my lady."

"Mrs. Tarrant, you should leave before he arrives. I do not want him to know you have any involvement in the diary's recovery. He should think only Gemma is looking for it. Join us this evening for dinner. I will inform the steward. You can apprise me of what you learn. Hopefully, you will have found the diary by then."

Isabella didn't have the same hope. "What should I do with the diary, if I find it?"

"Return it to Gemma."

"Is that wise?"

"My lady," the maid warned.

"I'm leaving," Isabella said and did so.

As the stateroom door closed, men's voices reached her, one which she recognized from last evening, the other with the barely-evident Greek accent that most of the stewards had. Isabella turned in the opposite direction, following the passageway to its turn. The corridor ended there, a short hall with one door at its end to access another cabin.

She peeked around the corner. A steward escorted Lord Stropeford to Lady Peverell's stateroom. He didn't knock but retreated to his post in the cross-corridor.

Stropeford stood at the door, staring at it. He glanced after the steward then looked toward the blind corridor. Isabella ducked back. Her heart hammered as she expected to hear footsteps approaching.

Then she heard a staccato knock. A door opened. She imagined Hettie Rufford's stoic face.

"My wife is visiting Lady Peverell."

"Lady Peverell will not receive additional visitors, my lord."

"Is my wife here? She said she would be. I escorted her here an hour ago. Has she left?" His voice spiraled into greater frustration with each statement.

"Lady Stropeford remains here, my lord."

"You said Lady Peverell is not receiving visitors. Gemma, there you are."

Isabella leaned against the wall and listened.

"I am not a visitor, Stropeford." Gemma sounded pedantic, a child reciting words she'd learned by rote. "Lady Peverell is like my grandmother. We said we would meet you at noon, in the Music Salon. You've interrupted Lady Peverell's toilette."

"You can come with me now."

"I will not. Lady Peverell wants my arm to the Music Salon."

"Gemma—."

Isabella heard a muted voice that could only be Lady Peverell, sounding like a querulous old woman. That redoubtable lady was far from querulous, questioning to discover what was happening. Lady Peverell dictated what happened. Isabella peeked around the corner again, to see Lord Stropeford and the hem of Hettie Rufford's dark uniform.

"We'll meet in the Music Salon as planned. Shut the door, Rufford," Gemma ordered. "We will be late for luncheon."

The door closed. Stropeford stared at the panel. His hands fisted at his sides. His bride had just refused his order. That had to be a first for him. Gemma's spine, though, depended upon Lady Peverell, not her own mettle. And Stropford didn't have the spine to push the issue. He turned on his heel and strode away.

Isabella counted 1,000 before she followed.

3

Rain peppered the decks, dotting her dress as Isabella dashed to the public areas marked for second- and third-class passengers.

Since noon rapidly approached, she headed for the dining hall. After last evening's luxurious dining room with glittering chandeliers, white linens and crystal, and fresh flowers on every table, the bare tables and stoneware plates were a strong reminder of the reality of her voyage. The food was heavy but bland, washed down by offered beer or tea. She chose tea, introduced herself to her tablemates, then gave a half-ear to their conversation about immigration to Australia while she puzzled over the previous half-hour.

Do I want to help Gemma Stropeford and Lady Peverell?

Maybe she should reverse that question. Her friend Cecilia had taught her several important lessons since their meeting last October, one of which was to act to benefit her own self before others. The important person to help in this instance was Lady Peverell. Restoring the diary to Gemma Stropeford would gain Lady Peverell's good will.

Gemma's plight did strike deep. Cecilia had been trapped in a loveless marriage. Before her late husband's death conveniently solved the divorce issue, Cecilia had anticipated years before she would be free to marry the man she loved.

Nor was Isabella certain she even liked Gemma. The younger woman was certainly naïve about the world. Her youth explained her flighty behavior and selfish intent. Too easily Isabella could cast disparaging words at the young bride. Her scattered conversation had thrown open the door to her interior closet, a jumble with few redeeming qualities.

Gemma fit well into the mad whirl that infected much of London's young society. The war over, they celebrated living without a care for any consequences to themselves. That hectic need for the next new experience had captured Cecilia for a time, until she broke away and finally realized hope for the future.

Did Gemma have any of that hope? She hadn't attempted loyalty to her new husband. She knew and had known for years that she wouldn't marry the man she claimed to love. She didn't deny herself what she wanted; she had only pursued what offered temporary happiness.

Although Isabella had only observed Douglas Stropeford twice, she knew he had a flawed personality. He berated his new wife in public. He'd thrown a letter and notes at her, yet he hadn't opened the letter. She couldn't determine if he had a temper or if extreme frustration with his wife drove him.

If he had the diary, why hadn't he confronted Gemma with it?

He hadn't ripped out the most damning pages. Was he holding those back? Waiting for an opportunity to confront his bride with them? Holding them as evidence for his lawyers? Then why had he claimed that he didn't want a divorce?

Those questions had too many missing pieces. Her brief was to find the diary.

Where would anyone hide it? Especially if that person didn't want it to be read? Would Stropeford trust his valet with it? Had someone else had access to it? The maid would have, but would the maid risk stealing the diary?

Who else had access to their stateroom?

Her first guess of the shipping office was a place to start. What was the best way to discover if Douglas Stropeford had mailed a package to London?

She ran a hand down her neat two-piece, a simple jacket and long skirt in slate blue, demure garb that she'd donned for the interview with Lady Peverell. The same attire should give her a professional look that might impress a clerk.

The postal station combined a mailing desk with a shipping office. Located on the third lower deck, the small anteroom was crowded by a long desk that separated the workers from the passengers who ventured there. A partial wall, with open doors to the back on either side, added to the separation.

A clerk stood ready at a central point behind the desk. Tall and thin, he had close-cut frizzy curls, grizzled with silver. The houndstooth clerk's jacket fit him loosely. He clasped his hands on a closed ledger. A two-inch stack of envelopes bound with twine rested beside him. Behind the partial wall, men talked, and things thumped.

She entered with a smile, which the clerk didn't return.

Subterfuge was needed. No mail clerk would answer a casual query about stamped mail or packages. Most of the *Nomadic's* stewards were Greek, and Isabella had won a bit more cordiality from them with the prep-school Greek her father had taught. The BAON line employed from across Europe, stewards from Greece with a scattering from other countries, chefs from France and Germany, and assistants from the Netherlands and Belgium and Italy. The clerks, though, with their paper-heavy work, were all from England, in keeping with the company's roots.

This man's appearance gave few clues to his origin. Clean-shaven, he wore a starched collar over his white shirt. Starched cuffs hung loosely at his wrists. His shoulders were squared. He looked a bastion of British clerkdom, and she had to besiege the very postal regulations he had vowed to uphold.

"Good afternoon, sir. Lady Peverell, in Stateroom 7, has sent me on an errand."

Nothing about the clerk's facial expression changed, not by a twitch or a blink. "May I inquire as to your name, ma'am?"

That was definitely an English accent, London polish with a Tyneside underlay. "Of course. I am Mrs. Madoc Tarrant. My berth is C 31. And your name, sir?"

One eyebrow rose at her unusual request. "August Clemmings. How may I assist Lady Peverell, Mrs. Tarrant?"

The Peverell name and influence in English society might be known to this man. Her hopes rose. "Lady Peverell wishes to know if you have received a package that her friend wished to have mailed."

The clerk frowned. "Postal regulations forbid the return of letters and packages once those are received and stamped for mailing."

Isabella let her smile falter. "I do realize this is an uncommon request. Lady Peverell does not wish to remove the package from mailing. She merely wishes to know that the package was received." Placing a hand on the desk, she leaned closer and confided, "You see, her friend's husband offered to mail the package, but her ladyship has no confidence that the task was performed."

Both of August Clemmings' eyebrows lowered. "I do wish that regulations allowed me to assist Lady Peverell. However—."

Before he continued with a refusal, Isabella added, "I would merely need to confirm the package's receipt. Do you have a logbook or a ledger to record receipt of such packages?" Her gaze fell to the ledger.

Clemmings hesitated then opened it. "What day would the package have been mailed?"

"Yesterday or the day before or the day before that. Lady Peverell did not say."

He opened to the last page with writing. "Perhaps the name of the person mailing the package?"

"Would it have that name if a servant mailed it for them?"

"One would certainly hope so." His pursed mouth gave a silent speech about the vagaries of clerks who attended the desk when August Clemmings was off-duty.

"The package was to be mailed by Lady Gemma Stropeford. Her husband is Lord Douglas Stropeford. I believe his servant is Henredon. Her maid is Tamman."

Clemmings ran his finger down the page. He turned back a page and did the same then did the next pages. "No. No packages or letters received from any of those names."

Her dismay did not have to faked. "There hasn't been? Oh dear. Are you certain?"

He flipped a third page, and she saw the tallied numbers at the bottom of columns. "This page is from our docking in Southhampton, before we started this voyage."

"Oh. The package would certainly not have been mailed before we came on board. Well." She gave a decided nod. "With your help, Mr. Clemmings, I have fulfilled my errand for Lady Peverell. The package has not been mailed."

"Do you have any other requests, Mrs. Tarrant?"

"No. Thank you for your assistance, Mr. Clemmings. Good day to you."

He closed the ledger and resumed his stance. "And to you, ma'am."

Isabella puzzled over the problem as she climbed to the first lower deck. The Silver Lounge was packed with everyone driven inside by the rain.

Not seeing anyone that she knew, she abandoned the lounge and ventured along the Silver Star passageway. She peeked into the Quiet Room, a salon for those not wanting the gaiety of the lounge. The locked library, little more than a cubicle, would be accessible only during morning hours. Rain had drenched the deck-side windows of the Sun Room. One couple looked around as she hovered in the doorway. The other couples were too involved in their conversations to notice. Isabella gave a cursory survey for hiding places before retreating.

A clatter of dishes in the dining hall bespoke stewards preparing for dinner service, and she remembered Lady Peverell's invitation to dinner. The rain soaked her as she darted along the deck for the stairs to the third-class berths.

A ship had hundreds of places to secrete a thin diary. She needed more information. She needed a better understanding of who had taken the diary. Gemma blamed her husband. Isabella disagreed.

Why was the diary taken? That was the crucial question. As evidence for a divorce, then yes, Lord Stropeford was the culprit. But the pages and letter he'd flung at his wife insinuated rather than proved. The notes on Gemma's breakfast tray were additional proof that someone possessed the diary.

The only reason for this morning's note was proof of possession, with a threat of more and worse to come.

The only reason to threaten Gemma was blackmail.

Gemma couldn't pay with pound notes, not aboard ship. Any letter to her banker, authorizing a withdrawal, could be stopped. Her only source of money was her jewelry.

Would the next torn-out page be accompanied by a blackmailer's request?

4

Dinner in the Gold Star dining room was far superior to her potato-based lunch in the Silver dining room.

The Stropefords had replaced the Gallaghers at table. In her introduction to the newcomers to the table, Lady Peverell underlined the point that Isabella was only now meeting Lady Gemma Stropeford. Isabella fell in with the plan even as she wondered how long that little lie would last. The younger woman's artless conversation with Sheridan Ingram might ruin all.

Col. Werthy had returned to the table. Colfax Ingram was missing, along with Mrs. Drake and Miss Swandon. In their place, at Lady Peverell's left, was Lionel Wexford. Across table were the missionary Miss Harlow and a Mrs. Bridgewater, who managed to keep the attentions of Hyatt Ingram, Col. Werthy, and Lord Stropeford through five courses.

By dinner's end, Isabella didn't think any of those three men felt neglected by the dashing widow. She could not say the same of Mr. Wexford's powers of conversation. Gemma Stropeford's big green eyes had certainly captivated Sheridan Ingram.

Isabella's conversation was reduced to Miss Harlow, an awkward cross-table around the center bouquet of white lilies and yellow roses. When the older woman discovered their berths were near each other, she found herself drafted to accompany Miss Harlow below-decks. She didn't manage a private word with Lady Peverell or Gemma. Since she had nothing of her own to report, that didn't concern her.

When she entered her room, Nedda Cortland was there, reading another glossy magazine. Hettie Rufford started up from her bunk.

"Slow down." Isabella slipped off her two-strapped heels and dropped her shawl on the lower bunk that was hers. "Lady Peverell has decided an evening of dancing with the Stropefords and Ingrams is required after she indulged in chocolate three times today."

Hettie sank back onto her upper bunk. "Thank heavens. She wore me to a frazzle this morning and was a curmudgeon all afternoon. Why did she want to see you?"

"That's what I want to ask you about. Apparently, Gemma Stropeford's diary has fallen into unscrupulous hands."

Hettie propped on her elbow. "Lady Stropeford? I never. That's the reason I had to search her stateroom this morning *and* this afternoon?"

"Is she being blackmailed?" Nedda asked.

"Not yet. I expect that's next."

Nedda returned to her magazine.

"Why did they call for you?" Hettie asked.

"I'm to find the missing diary."

"An impossible task," Nedda opined, proving that she was listening although her gaze remained glued to the gaily-dressed models.

"Perhaps not. I've been wondering how anyone would be able to take a diary that's kept in a first-class passenger's vanity case."

Nedda frowned. "They couldn't. At least, not just anyone could. Mr. Ingram's valet remains in his stateroom when the maid comes in to clean and change the linens."

"As do I," Hettie murmured.

"When did Lady Stropeford last have her diary?"

"After we left La Rochelle. She writes the previous day's events as she has her morning tea," Isabella explained. "Last night her husband confronted her with two pages torn from the diary. This morning she had another torn page on her breakfast tray. Lord Stropeford also had her letter that should have been mailed. How did he come by that letter?"

Hettie gave a shamed face. "He caught me with it, as I was taking it to be mailed."

"How did he know to look for it?"

"Lord Stropeford's wits do not impress," Nedda drawled. "Mr. Ingram can still run rings around the man."

"Someone told him." Isabella tapped a finger on her chin. "Did Lady Stropeford receive any notes this afternoon?"

"I wouldn't know."

"What do you know of her maid?"

"Tamman? She came with the marriage."

"The Farradays employed her?"

"No. She was hired for Lady Stropeford when the betrothal settlements were agreed upon."

"What do *you* think of Tamman, Hettie?"

The maid shrugged. "She does her job well."

That answer was no help. Isabella wanted to know the maid's potential loyalty. A flash of insight struck. "Do you do a job, Hettie, or do you serve Lady Peverell?"

"I serve her ladyship."

"Ah." Nedda cast her magazine aside. "That's clever of you, Isabella."

"A lucky guess. So, this Tamman has no real loyalty to Lady Stropeford."

"Nor does that valet Henredon," Hettie snapped. "This very afternoon I caught him sneaking around the first-class salons. He jumped out of his shoes when he saw me carrying her ladyship's shawl."

"He knows you work for Lady Peverell?"

"Of course he knows. We traveled in the same compartment from London to Southhampton. He and that Tamman had their heads together the whole train trip."

"Then this Henredon also knows that Lady Peverell is like a godmother to Lady Stropeford, and he likely knows by now that Lady Peverell knows the diary is missing and will take action to protect her." Isabella sank onto her bunk. "We dock mid-morning tomorrow in Gibraltar, a proper dock, not just a tug coming out with packages and supplies."

Nedda caught her idea. "It will be their first opportunity to leave the ship. But will they?"

"Malta is five days from here. It's leave now or risk being discovered and tossed in a brig until the next port."

"They've gained nothing yet. There's been no blackmail."

Isabella bit her lip. "Still—. A lot can happen in a few hours. And I still haven't found the diary. Hettie, where was Henredon when you saw him? By which salons? The library? The Reading Room?"

"The lounge. The library. Oh, and the Music Salon."

"Where better to keep a stolen diary than away from your own things?" Nedda offered softly.

"Where better to stow it than in an unexpected place? No one will look for a book in the Music Salon." The image blazed in her mind: sorting through the music sheets stored in the piano bench or on the music stand, seeing a slim diary at the bottom. After a brief glimpse inside, someone intent on song sheets would ignore it.

She stood up and slipped on her evening heels then tossed the paisley shawl over her black dress.

"When you don't return," Nedda asked, "where shall I tell them to find the body? The first-class library?"

"The Music Salon."

5

The diary wasn't in the Music Salon. It was in the library—although she nearly didn't find it.

The sleepy steward smiled at her faltering school-girl Greek and let her take her time to browse the shelves. The selection was hundreds of books better than the Silver Star library. Impatience rose higher with each shelf, and Isabella considered checking behind every book.

Then she spotted it, more amber than orange, a half-inch thick, and packed with all a young woman's dreams and follies. It nestled between two thick books in a far corner on a bottom shelf, a book hidden among books, like Edgar Allan Poe's purloined letter, a story only an American would know.

Isabella's hand shook as she drew it from the shelf. When she carried it to the clerk, he looked for the ship stamp. Not finding it, he shrugged and gave it back. "No checkout needed," he said. She counted that a small blessing, for she doubted a third-class passenger would be allowed a first-class library's book.

Holding it against her breast, she headed for the main deck.

The rain had stopped. A brisk wind played havoc with her hair, her shawl, and her skirts. *Cry havoc*, she thought and turned toward Lady Peverell's stateroom.

A dark figure separated from the wall beside the stair. "What you have is mine," he ground out.

The American accent was a stark contrast to the British accents she'd heard since before the Great War. No wonder he'd used the library to hide the diary. "Henredon?" she guessed.

"Give it to me."

Isabella sidestepped to the railing.

The valet followed. "We knew you'd be after the diary. Lady Stropeford told Tamman, idiot that she is. Hand it over now, or—."

"Or what?" came a smooth voice behind Isabella.

Henredon jerked back. She put her back to the railing and glanced behind her.

Col. Werthy's cigarillo tip glowed red as he inhaled. "I'm waiting." The innocuous words had an ominous growl.

The valet stepped back into the shadows. Footsteps clanged as he ran down the outer stairs.

"Well, Mrs. Tarrant?"

"Colonel." She settled on simple words. "Thank you."

"An escort would be wise, this late at night."

"I will remember that."

"May I escort you somewhere?"

Isabella hesitated. "Should we report him?"

"I daresay he'll debark at Gibraltar."

"Yes, but—." She hesitated. She didn't have permission to share the story of the diary far and wide. She thought she could trust Nedda and Hettie, but the colonel? No. And no crime had been committed, just the threat of a crime, to Gemma and to herself. Henredon had prepared for blackmail, but she'd found the diary before he used it for that.

If she returned the diary to Gemma or to Lady Peverell, how long before it once again went *missing*?

She flung the diary over the railing. Wind fluttered the pages as the diary dropped. The gust also played havoc with her shawl. She snatched the cloth before it flew away. Far below came a faint splash, almost lost in the wind and the waves that the ship ploughed through.

"A simple solution," Werthy commented. "For the best, I've always found." He exhaled, and the rich tobacco scent surrounded her before it also whisked away.

"May I have your arm? I must speak with Lady Peverell."

"And Lady Stropeford?"

How much did Col. Werthy know? Rather than question him, she held out her hand. "I will leave it to her ladyship to explain to her protégée."

He offered his crooked elbow.

6

To Lady Peverell Isabella said only that she had disposed of the diary, witnessed by Col. Werthy. She implied that the valet was not a good choice for an employee.

The older woman gave her a gimlet eye. "I doubt we'll convince Stropeford to do without a valet."

"I may have an answer to that," Werthy said. "Ah, our young bride. Lady Stropeford, may I have the next dance?" Gemma giggled and grabbed his offered hand. "Lady Peverell," he bowed slightly, "at your service." Then he was towed onto the dance floor.

And Isabella stole away, satisfied that she had completed a mission she hadn't asked for or wanted.

In the morning, brilliant sunshine had replaced the dreary rainclouds. With the excitement of docking and the scurrying haste of stewards, the toiling sailors and swarming dock workers, no one noticed that two servants with packed bags were first off-ship when the gangplank was positioned.

Only when Lord Stropeford returned from the gymnasium did he discover his valet had disappeared, along with his wallet of ready cash.

Lady Stropeford called and called for her maid, but she had also vanished, taking a jewelry case that Lord Stropeford had given his wife upon their marriage.

Captain Pitney escorted the couple to the local authorities to file a report for one Edgar Allan Henredon and one Elspeth Tamman.

When that hullaballoo died down, Isabella did ask Lady Peverell to send a "thank you" to August Clemmings in the mail room.

On the dock, Col. Werthy paused to light his cigarillo. Passengers streamed past, intent on exploring the town before they returned late in the afternoon. He shook out the match then offered an arm to Isabella. "We won't venture to the Spanish border, Mrs. Tarrant, unlike others who will be unnamed. Now, before us is the great Rock of Gibraltar."

Purple Poison

1

"What will your husband think of your flirtation with Colonel Werthy?"

Isabella stared at that single line scrawled across the cream-colored sheet of paper. Blinding sunlight flashed in her eyes. She blinked, and the words in purple wavered on the page.

What will Madoc think?

Her husband would have nothing to think, nothing to suspect. She *wasn't* flirting with the colonel. They had explored Gibraltar Town and Athens together. They dined together nightly, at Mr. Ingram's table, the only regulars beside Lady Peverell and Sheridan Ingram. Even Mr. Ingram's grandson Colfax appeared once in three days. Sometimes they did stroll the Promenade or reserved deck chairs side-by-side.

That wasn't a flirtation, merely friendship of two similar minds. The colonel could talk art. She knew more than a little about world politics, currently and historically. Their association was nothing more than that.

A figure crossed before her, blocking the brilliant Mediterranean sun before dropping into the chaise beside hers. "You're frowning, Mrs. Tarrant."

The very man in question, Col. Werthy looked the gentleman at leisure in a summer suit, straw boater, and diagonally striped Repp tie. She waited until he had lit one of his ubiquitous cigarillos then handed over the letter.

He scanned it before those glass-clear grey eyes met hers. "I didn't expect you to be the next target. My apologies."

"The next target? Other people have received letters like this?" Even as she asked, Isabella considered potential recipients. One of those would not be Gemma Stropeford with her missing diary. She and her husband had debarked in Gibraltar, deciding their better course would be a return to England. Isabella had admitted to some relief as they left ship, aided by a loan from Lady Peverell. She had not wanted to become either confidante or good friend to

Gemma.

Werthy waved the single sheet. "You join a privileged circle. I know of three others. No doubt more clutch their poison pen letters close, trying to hide them."

"Poison pen?"

"What else would you call this? It's a mild version compared to others that I've seen, but it's clearly designed to poison your emotions."

"A mild version? Did you receive one?"

"Not I. I had opportunity to read one."

"A single line like this?"

"Rather longer. Quite the diatribe."

"Really?" She wanted to ask *who else?* and *what was in the letter?*, but those questions seemed the height of rudeness.

He drew on the thin dark cigar, and she caught a whiff of rich tobacco under the smoke. "Mrs. Tarrant, you didn't ask the expected question."

"I didn't? But we're not involved in a flirtation, are we?"

Werthy chuckled. "You never fail to surprise me. Are you not going to demand that I absent myself from your company?"

"I will not. This claim lacks proof." She held out her hand, and he returned the letter with its vicious implication.

"No worries about what your husband will think?"

"I am innocent of any flirtation. Besides, they would need to know Madoc's address in India. I doubt they do—unless they've invaded my cabin and absconded with one of his letters. Nor do I think they will travel all the way to Madras and personally inform him of my supposed perfidy."

Laughter from three youths strolling past broke Isabella's attention on the letter. Her gaze traveled along the crowded Promenade deck. Anyone could have written the letter.

No, not anyone. Only someone who knew she was married could have penned it, someone who'd seen her growing friendship with Col. Werthy, someone who wanted to poison that friendship.

Farther along the deck, in the chaises, she saw Mrs. Phoebe Drake, dark head bent over a fashion magazine. A few chairs on, Miss Arabella Swandon manipulated a hook in and out of a handwork project. The ecru string reminded Isabella of a fisherman's sweater. The Gallaghers and their daughter stood at the ship rail, Mrs. Gallagher holding a wide-brimmed straw hat firmly on her head, the ribbon around her daughter's boater fluttering in the breeze. A young woman with golden curls, shining in the Mediterranean sun, looked their way. When her gaze encountered Isabella's, she ducked her head and hid behind a novel.

Isabella looked again at the scrawl of purple ink. The handwriting was upright, the words open and well-spaced, the letters formed loosely, the capital W's and C tall and lean. It certainly didn't look like the hand of a poisonous person. Only Werthy's name was stated, not hers, and she was not the only woman to receive his attentions. The note had no date. At the top was the ship's seal, engraved in gold, stationery from a first-class salon.

Isabella refolded the letter and slipped it inside its envelope, also with a gold seal. Here was her name, the M of Mrs. open with a waved hook for its start, the I of Isabella a tall line hooked at the bottom, the T with a hooked line at the top then straight down. The pen had torn a hole in the envelope when the nib crossed the last T in Tarrant. Here was the evidence of enmity and an angry heart.

"Tell me what you know, Colonel."

"Now that sounds like a determined mind."

A smile tugged at the corner of his mouth. He held his cigarillo over the chaise arm. The smoke wafted away from them. In that silence, something—the lines around his eyes, a vagrant intonation half-sensed—something caught her attention, and Isabella gave him a sharper look.

Col. Werthy had the lean athletic grace that made her think of a mountain lion seen at the zoo in Philadelphia. Attention to his attire gave him a sharp mien echoed in his military bearing. He never set himself forward, but he was a presence that couldn't be overlooked. Sheridan Ingram had disclosed that he saw Werthy in the ship's gymnasium whenever he managed to attend. He had the good graces of Lady Peverell, that redoubtable scion of nobility, as well as Hyatt Ingram, wealthy financier. They both cut through pretensions like a sharp blade through butter.

His smile dropped. "The artist's eye," he murmured. "That risk I didn't expect."

Isabella felt a pang at that implied slight to her talent, and her voice sharpened. "Because I paint pretty landscapes and avoid sketching my fellow passengers?"

Rather than answer, he looked away, his gaze following people strolling the deck or standing in conversation.

She spotted the dilettante Lionel Wexford talking to a young man clad in a fisherman's striped shirt. Farther along the railing a mutton-chopped elderly gentleman stared at a gull diving around the one of the ship's four masts.

She broke the stretching silence. "Will this change things between us? Will it change our friendship? Are we going to change over one line in purple ink?"

Those clear grey eyes returned to her. He had his own artist's eye, piercing beyond the obvious, and she feared he saw just how much she enjoyed their relationship. He smiled and infused warmth into his answer. "No. No, Mrs. Tarrant, we aren't."

Yet she mistrusted that forced heartiness. Isabella tucked the letter in her sketchbook then swivelled her legs off the chaise. "Walk with me."

The breeze ruffled her hair. The skirt of her blue polka-dot dress fluttered around her ankles. If she could walk him away from everyone else, where they wouldn't be overheard, he might tell her about the other recipients. If she knew about them, she might be able to find a common link.

The vivid blue sky was bright against the dark blue waters surging around the ship. They passed a couple strolling the deck, arms linked and heads bent to each other, a mother herding a daughter and son away from the shuffle board game played by two teenaged boys, a man walking alone, and two young women chatting and giggling.

As they neared the bow, Isabella veered toward the railing. Out from under the upper deck and against the rail, the sun was brilliant and the the wind stronger. Her skirts tangled around the railing, reaching for the sea. Overhead the sky was a blue haze, but far to the east, storm clouds threatened the waters that they sailed toward.

Werthy took off his boater and stared at the distant clouds. The wind ruffled his dark, wavy hair. It tore his tie from his linen jacket, and the striped ends streamed across his chest.

No one was within fifteen feet of them, and no one seemed to watch them. Now was the time to ask the important questions. "Who else? Who else has received a letter?"

Werthy gave a cutting gesture.

Isabella huffed. "You said three others were in this privileged circle of recipients. Will you tell me who they are? Do you know how long ago these letters started?"

He raised an eyebrow. "You think to investigate?"

"I think a minor evil unchecked will turn into a greater evil. Did we not just fight a war with a minor cause that exploded into a major issue?"

"A hit, a palpable hit," he quoted *Hamlet* and touched a finger to his brow. Those literary injections and his wide-ranging knowledge of his world were two reasons she valued his company. "I have no first-hand knowledge of those letters. Nor do I have permission to name the third."

"You've piqued my curiosity, Colonel, but I will not censure you for discretion. I did not come on this voyage to poke my nose into other people's business."

His gaze swept the deck, tracking their walk past the shuffle board game and back to the deck chairs. He eyed the closest person, a lady swathed in a shawl, her attention was on the teenagers shouting over the shuffleboard game. "Join me for luncheon," he finally said. "You may find it edifying."

Luncheon was out. As much as Isabella wanted answers, she wouldn't disappoint a friend. "I regret that I have another invitation, but I thank you."

"Lady Peverell?"

"Not today, no."

"Nedda Cortland?"

Now what did Col. Werthy know about Hyatt Ingram's personal secretary? "The very same," she murmured. She would not tease the information from him. He would either share it or not. She stepped away from the railing, preparing to depart.

"Bring her with you. No doubt she will prefer a Gold Star luncheon to a mere Silver Star. Or does she enjoy her half-hour snatched away from her employer?"

"If she consents" was all that Isabella would commit to.

2

Because she wanted to drop her sketchbook in her cabin, Isabella detoured to drop it on her bunk. She rushed to the Silver Star dining room, knowing Nedda would be waiting for her. Yet with the clatter of dishes loud in the passageway to the dining room, she thought to share the letter with Nedda. She hastened back, out of breath when she burst into the cabin.

A maid straightened from Isabella's bunk. She jerked the top sheet from the bed.

"Oh!" Isabella exclaimed, surprised to see the young woman. "Do excuse me. I need my sketchbook," but it had disappeared from the bed. "There was a book here. Did you see it?"

"Yes, miss. I placed it there." The maid pointed to the washstand.

Isabella retrieved it and opened it to find the letter. It was gone. She flipped through the pages then shook the open book over the sink, but no letter fell out. She glanced around but saw nothing on the floor. "Did you see a letter addressed to me? I'm Mrs. Madoc Tarrant."

"No, miss." She tugged at another sheet to pull it off the thin mattress and dropped it onto the floor.

"Any letter at all?"

"No, miss."

Isabella balanced the sketchbook on the washstand. "I had a letter here."

The maid stripped the blanket from Nedda's bunk. The cotton blanket muffled her words. "I've not seen a letter, miss."

The letter might have fallen out as she rushed down to the cabin. Yet she'd held the sketchbook closed. Could anything have fluttered out?

She remembered the wind's force as she stood by the railing. Could the letter have slipped from the sketchbook then? Surely she would have seen it flying away?

What other way could the letter have gone missing? Several minutes had passed between dropping off the sketchbook and her return. The trek from third-class to the second-class public rooms required several passageways and two stairs. "Has anyone else been here?"

"No, miss. Was the letter important?" The maid dropped another sheet onto the pile between the bunks.

"No, not at all." She wouldn't forget that single line of poison in purple ink. And she didn't intend to investigate. *Other people's letters are not my business*, she firmly decided as she ventured back to the Silver Star dining room.

Nedda was already there, claiming a seat at the head of a table. At the other end was the family immigrating to Australia. Nedda waved then broke apart her roll to butter it as Isabella joined the queue to receive her tray. A rice mélange of green peas, chopped carrots, and chicken with limp green beans to the side and a tomato soup as thin as broth made her regret refusing Col. Werthy's invitation.

"You're late," Nedda said as she slid onto the straight-backed chair.

"My apologies. I wish I hadn't been delayed. We received an invitation to a Gold Star luncheon."

Nedda wordlessly looked at her meal then lifted her eyes skyward. "I'm free this half-hour. There, I might not be. Mr. Ingram might think me available for more dictation, and I don't wear my steno pad and pen. Who invited you to luncheon? Lady Peverell? Is she increasing her sheltering wing over you?"

"The invitation came from Col. Werthy."

The secretary's mouth dropped open.

"I have a greater surprise. I received a letter. A poison pen letter."

"You, too?"

"You've received one?"

"Not I," Nedda declared and tried to spear a green bean. "Sheridan Ingram. I don't know what it said, but Mr. Ingram descended into one of his tirades. 'Can you not control yourself for three weeks?'" she shared in a deepened voice. "I tried to close my ears and become invisible."

"Which never works."

"No, it doesn't. What did your letter say?"

"Just one line. *What will your husband think of your flirtation with Col. Werthy?* Was Sheridan Ingram's letter written in purple ink?"

"Yes. I had to pick up the pieces off the floor. Mr. Ingram tore it into little pieces. Is that all? His letter was substantially longer than a single line."

"Do you know what it said?"

"Kisses in the dark," she quoted. "Seen leaving. Adulterous."

"Any names?"

Nedda shook her head and tried another green bean. "I didn't want Mr. Ingram to think I was piecing the letter together."

"I do suppose a wise secretary knows when to be blind." She tried the rice mélange then looked for the salt shaker. "Col. Werthy says he knows three recipients of these letters."

"Four, with you."

"Four? Yes. Is Sheridan Ingram a fifth? When did he receive his letter?"

"Over the weekend. I don't think he immediately informed his father that he'd received it."

"What would prompt hm to tell his father? Another letter?" Nedda merely shrugged. Isabella leaned forward and lowered her voice. "Here's the interesting thing. I tucked the letter in my sketchbook and took it to our cabin. As I came here, I realized that I wanted you to see it, so I went back. A maid was there, stripping the beds. The letter was gone."

"Gone? Did you drop it?"

"No, I couldn't have."

"The maid took it?"

"She says not."

"Curiouser and curiouser."

The steward arrived with small bowls of dessert, a whipped mousse that looked large but was primarily foamy air.

Nedda checked the watch pinned to the lapel of her tailored charcoal jacket. "Mr. Ingram will be looking for me. He is re-thinking, yet again, his approach to the Bahrain sheikh. These petroleum rights are stressing him, and he's stressing me." She sighed eloquently. "What will you do this afternoon?"

"I wanted to start another watercolor of a coastline. We'll reach Port Said in two more days."

"I think you should discover who received these letters and look for any commonality. Are the letters restricted to first-class passengers? We're third-class, but you dine every evening with Lady Peverell and the Ingrams. Whoever writes these letters may not know you're not in first-class."

"The letters are directed against the first-class passengers? That would make the writer also a first-class passenger."

Nedda shrugged. "I'm off." She gave a jaundiced eye at the remains of Isabella's dessert. "Enjoy your foam."

The foamy mousse cleansed the palate but little more. Finishing her tea, Isabella considered the situation. She knew only that poison pen letters were being sent. Hers was a single line while Sheridan Ingram had a whole page. Why that difference? *Am I a late addition for this writer? Do they not know enough about me to write more than one line?*

She returned to her cabin to collect her watercolors.

The sheets were still bundled on the floor, her bed and Nedda's stripped to the mattress. The maid had abandoned her work.

Maybe that hadn't been a maid but someone sent to retrieve Isabella's letter.

Had the letter writer sent the maid? Or was the maid the letter writer?

Isabella wished she had paid more attention to the woman. All she could remember of her appearance was that she was neither young nor old. She'd worn the maid's uniform, a drab chambray with a darker apron and a kerchief covering her hair, the same dark blue as the apron.

When she asked the steward about a maid refreshing the bed linens, he frowned over her question. "Not until we dock in Egypt." He had seen a maid in the passageways, but he had ignored her. The woman had carried a tray from dining. "Perhaps, Mrs. Tarrant, if you ask there?"

Isabella knew that no answer would come from dining. The woman had chosen a clever disguise.

Remaking the beds, Isabella ran through her questions. Why had the woman wanted to retrieve that letter?

Had the woman targeted first-class, and discovering Isabella belonged to third-class, she removed it?

Had she intended it for someone else and sent it to Isabella for spite? Then why retrieve it?

She didn't know enough for answers. With the letter gone, she wasn't certain she should seek any answers.

Sketchbook in hand, she headed for the Promenade deck, hoping to cast the problem out of her head.

3

That evening's dinner added to Isabella's questions.

She arrived second to the table. The elderly Miss Swandon was first, a shawl over her bronze gown. The *maître d'* placed Isabella on the same side as the older woman, an empty chair between them. With the intervening man not yet present, conversation would be easy.

Isabella smiled and introduced the weather. When the sunny day and light breeze exhausted that topic, she asked about the woman's current project. "I saw you on deck earlier, working away. Your hook looked rather long. Aren't most crochet hooks about five inches or so?" There, she'd contributed the breadth of her knowledge about handwork.

"My current project requires that long hook. It's worked in Tunisian crochet, sometimes called the Princess Frederick William stitch or the Princess Royal stitch. I've even heard it as *Ecossais tricoter*. *Tricoter* is French for knitting. This mantle," she touched the ombre beige shawl, "is in Tunisian crochet." A faint stain marred the side of her left finger.

"The fabric you create looks very much like knitting. How did you learn it?"

"A neighbor taught me, while my office was stationed in France, early in the war. I prefer this type of crochet to other stitches, for the work is never turned. We have a forward pass, leaving all stitches on the hook, then we pass back, casting off as we work each stitch."

"I've never heard of Tunisian crochet. Granted, I know very little about crochet or knitting."

Miss Swandon sniffed. "You are devoted to your art, dear." Her tone gave *art* capital letters, "and very good you are with it. Who is that youngish woman I've seen occasionally accompany you on deck, Mrs. Tarrant?"

"I believe you mean Miss Nedda Cortland. She and I share a cabin with two other young ladies."

The woman shuddered. "My, the trials of third class. Have I seen her with the elder Mr. Ingram?"

"Nedda is his personal secretary."

Miss Swandon nodded. "Well do I know the life of a personal secretary."

"That was your former position?"

"Indeed. For many years I was secretary to an unassuming man who made grave decisions every hour of every day. He paid me handsomely. I didn't quite know what to do with myself when I had to retire from that position after the war. I booked this trip at his suggestion. We *are* early to dinner, aren't we? I expected you to come in on Col. Werthy's arm. You are so often together."

Isabella's gaze sharpened. *Did Miss Swandon write that letter?* Yet she saw nothing new in the elderly woman's façade. She was the spinster incarnate: wispy silver hair escaping a tight bun, watery blue eyes, the wrinkles of age, a *pince-nez* on a ribbon about her neck but never used, her clothes well made but far behind fashion. The shawl enveloped her thin shoulders, swaddling her even though the room wasn't chilled.

"Col. Werthy and I have common interest in history and world events, which was my father's speciality."

"He's not quite the man with whom you should associate." Before Isabella could decode that statement, Miss Swandon said with delight, "Here are the Ingrams."

Hyatt Ingram greeted them as he took his usual host's position. Following him was a couple new to the table. Mr. and Mrs. Nevil Fremont looked like middle-aged gentry long settled into complacency. Their daughter Savina Fremont, a golden-curled beauty with bright red lipstick and slanted brown eyes, came on Sheridan Ingram's arm.

Ingram younger placed himself to the hostess right, with Miss Fremont at his side. His quiet remarks had her giggling and casting coquettish glances while the Ingram elder focused on Mrs. Fremont, a dowdy woman eclipsed by the double strand of pearls across her ample bosom.

Escorting Lady Peverell was Padgett Michaels, a non-descript man who had little to say. He took the chair between Isabella and Miss Swandon. The spinster quickly engaged him in conversation about the bazaar she'd explored when they docked in Rhodes, leaving Isabella with nothing to do but listen to the various conversations.

Last to come, missing the cocktail but sliding into his seat as the steward served a cream soup, was Col. Werthy. He gave his apologies to the table at large then preceded to charm Miss Fremont's attentions away from Sheridan Ingram.

"They toured Valetta together," Mr. Michaels muttered in Isabella's ear.

"I beg your pardon?"

He nodded to indicate the lively conversation across the table. "When we were docked at Malta. The Fremonts wanted an escort to tour the Old Town, and Lady Peverell recommended the colonel."

"And did you tour Valetta?"

"I had business in the Old Town, part of my reason for this trip. I did see you and your friend, though."

"Nedda Cortland. Mr. Ingram had no need of a secretary that day."

"I never see her here, at dinner."

"Nedda guards her free time, Mr. Michaels."

"Whilst you are care-free."

"I set my own working hours. And you, Mr. Michaels? What is your business?"

"Antique jewelry, oddities and collectibles. I'm looking forward to our stay in Egypt. I expect to procure several finds in Cairo," and he spent the rest of the dinner describing exotics finds he had purchased in bazaars in Egypt and Arabia. He soon had her wishing she had signed up for the side excursions to Cairo, the pyramids at Giza, and Alexandria.

As they exited the dining room, Lady Peverell veered the women into a retiring salon. Isabella welcomed the delay. While the others would dance or play bridge, she would spend the rest of the evening in her cramped berth.

Miss Fremont sidled over to her. "You will not be dancing with us?"

"I prefer not to," although she would dearly love a late stroll on the decks or an evening playing cards rather than improving her mind with a book. Never invited, she didn't push herself into that group.

"I love dancing," the young woman enthused. "With some partners, I feel light as a feather. Do you dance with your husband?"

"We have. He does make me feel light although I will never quite be a featherweight."

Savina Fremont turned to the mirror and touched her curls. "Do you miss him?"

"More than I dreamed that I would."

"Where is he now? Where will you meet him?"

"Madras." When the beauty looked blank, Isabella clarified, "That's India, on the other side of the subcontinent from Bombay. To where are you and your parents traveling?"

"Sri Lanka. Hong Kong. Then Hawaii and San Francisco and New York. All before we return to London."

Those places were greatly distant, requiring days upon days of travel, and Savina rattled them off as if they were stops on a train line. "I'm a little envious of your world tour. You will see many exotic places."

Savina dug into her beaded purse. "I hope they're more interesting than that ruined marble hall on the hill in Athens." Out came a gold lipstick case. The lipstick was a bright carnelian, stark against her creamy skin.

Did she mean the Parthenon? Or The Acropolis?

"Pater said it was important to see, and see it we must. We'll see the pyramids in Egypt, too. I hope they are more interesting."

Isabella doubted the young woman would find them so. She decided to change the subject. "That's a lovely frock you're wearing."

Without taking her eyes from the mirror, she popped the lipstick closed, dropped it in her purse, then snapped the clasp. She gave a wiggle, and the soft gold moiré shimmered in the low light. Seed pearls adorned the fragile lace draping the bodice while a Rhinestone ornament clasped the front waist, creating shape for the tubular gown. "A Callot Soeur original. A gown to make a man fall in love."

"A gown to make every woman envious."

Savina smiled. Miss Swandon appeared, fussing with her crocheted mantle. In the inner room, Mrs. Fremont spoke to the attendant.

"Col. Werthy is exceptionally nice, isn't he, Mrs. Tarrant?"

Isabella opened her eyes wide. She shot a glance to Miss Swandon and the other ladies waiting in the antechamber, but they hadn't heard Savina. With that single line of the letter glaring in her memory, she managed, "He has been a boon to this sole traveler."

Mrs. Fremont emerged, Lady Peverell behind her. "Come along," the dowager said. "You are needed this evening, Isabella. How are you at bridge?"

"Neither bad nor good," she said promptly, wanting to avoid her cabin as long as possible.

"You will make our fourth."

Card play occurred in the salon next to the ballroom. Several people had already started their games. Lady Peverell barely introduced Isabella to the older gentlemen obviously waiting for them. She partnered Mr. Fullerton, a man with old-fashioned mutton chops. They were soundly trounced by Lady Peverell and her partner, a Clive Rexford who shuffled and dealt with neat precision.

Music from the ballroom drifted in, accompaniment to shuffled cards, quiet bids, and occasional cries of triumph for an unexpected trick. By evening's end, Lady Peverell looked pleased and Mr. Rexford satisfied. Isabella was happy that the game's play had not depended on money. Mr. Fullerton was the only one displeased, and he left as soon as possible after they tallied points.

"Better than I expected," Isabella replied to Mr. Rexford's query about the evening. He smiled, pocketed the notebook in which he'd kept the tally, then bid them "Good evening" before strolling away.

"Your arm," Lady Peverell commanded, and Isabella complied. The hour seemed very late, and the dowager reminisced about several well-played rubbers. Her pace slowed as they walked the last passageway to her stateroom. "You will not pursue the acquaintance, Isabella."

Perplexed, she stared at the woman.

"There's some trouble in her background," the dowager added. "I cannot divine what. It's dangerous, whatever it is. They are keeping it very quiet. Here we are," she announced unnecessarily as the stateroom door opened, revealing the maid Hettie Rufford. "I am tired, Rufford."

"Too much excitement, my lady."

"She won all the tricks," Isabella said.

"Thank you, my dear. I want my tisane, Rufford."

"I have it ready, my lady," and the maid shut the door.

Her and *they*. She could only guess that Lady Peverell meant Savina and her parents.

4

In the rising warmth of the morning, the sea wind abated, and Isabella relished the lack of chill in the air.

She rapidly walked the Promenade Deck, hoping the exercise would clarify her questions or at least distract her from the letter and Lady Peverell's cryptic comment.

Dark clouds hovered on the distant horizon. The *Nomadic* steamed calmly toward the storm. Ahead was another long evening at sea, with Port Said still a day before them. The sea stretched endlessly around them, the waves ever restless, the breeze vagrant or gusty by turns, the sky a blue haze that changed only for sunset, sunrise, and the deep velvet night with sparkling stars.

She looked forward to their nine days docked in Port Said. The excursions looked more attractive with each day on board ship. The side trips cost additional money she hadn't budgeted, but she might sign for one excursion, to the pyramids, just to escape the ship for a week. The bulk of the voyage, confined to the ship with few ports for long visits, still remained before her.

The purser would have more details about the excursions. His answers might help her decide. Nedda was going; Mr. Ingram wanted his grandson to see the pyramids and required his secretary to be at hand, ready for dictation. The Ingrams, with Nedda and valets in tow, would leave the *Nomadic* later, at Muscat, Oman. They were off to venture to Bahrain and negotiations with the ruling sheik. Muscat would be some six days after the ship left Port Said.

Isabella turned back to find the Purser's Office.

A tall man with striking blond looks stopped abruptly. Giving a shake of his square head, he approached, stopping a few feet away. "Mrs. Tarrant? Mrs. Madoc Tarrant?"

Surprised that a stranger had approached, she noted the people around, walking their daily promenade. They looked to be a mix of second- and third-class passengers, even one swathed in a white shawl. This sun-bronzed demigod looked first-class. She didn't recognize him from the dining room, her sole steady entrée to the Gold Star world, but he might choose the later seating. Lady Peverell and the Ingrams preferred to dine at seven o'clock. First-class dining also offered a cozier seating at ten o'clock for the night owls who danced until the small hours.

He took a step nearer. "Mrs. Tarrant?"

No pouches beneath those clear blue eyes gave evidence of dissipation. His linen suit was neatly pressed, his tie sharply knotted, and his shoes shined to a gloss. He looked safe enough.

"You have the advantage of me, sir."

"My apologies, ma'am. Richard Owen, Devonshire. Col. Werthy described you and offered that you were often on the deck morning and afternoon. He said you would be painting or sketching?"

That rising question asked for a confirmation. *He's cautious. Why?* "My plans today were disrupted." He didn't need to know the reason.

"Would you walk with me, Mrs. Tarrant? The colonel gave me to understand that you would be interested in my—a current circumstance."

His formality added reassurance. Isabella nodded and turned away from the main salons and stairs, wanting the deck less crowded. Richard Owen came to her side quickly. She expected him to launch into his *circumstance*—a letter, she guessed—but he only walked, hands clasped behind him. After several yards continued in silence, she asked, "You are a friend of Col. Werthy, Mr. Owen?"

"Of long standing, Mrs. Tarrant. From the war. Artillery."

Werthy had never offered his war record, but she didn't think he was an artillery man. Sniper would be her guess, behind the lines, relying on his wits. She doubted Mr. Owen was artillery, but that meant nothing at this moment.

"Your circumstance, Mr. Owen?" she prompted. "Dare I ask if it concerns a letter?"

"It does. Werthy said you needed more evidence to investigate."

"I hadn't planned to investigate."

"Werthy said you would. You solved that murder Lady Peverell talked about, the one at the Malvaise estate."

She hoped no one ever discovered that she'd visited Crete and Upper Wellsford at the time murders had also occurred. "I didn't solve that murder. Truly I didn't. It solved itself. I was just there."

"And you helped Lady Stropeford."

"I wasn't aware—."

"No one knows exactly what happened," he spoke over her faint protest, "but Werthy said you had a neat solution to the problem. Not your fault the Stropefords had to leave the ship at Gibraltar." He reached into his jacket and produced the envelope she had dreaded. "Here it is. Read it." His extended arm, handing over the letter, blocked her advance.

Isabella stopped and reluctantly took it.

The envelope had the gold ship's seal in the corner, same as hers had had. *Richard Owen* was written across the front in purple ink. The capital R and O were not tall.

She slipped the letter out. The stationery had come from the same first-class salon. Here, though, the letters were completely different, her single line compared to a page of rancor for him. The words were open and well-spaced, but any comparison of the handwriting ended there. Her letter had vanished, but she had a vivid memory of loosely formed letters with a hooked swoop. This writing was slanted, the words dashed off. The T's had a long crossing line, the length of the word in several instances: *treachery* and *tolerable*, *contemptible* and *betrayal*, while *utterly* ventured into *despicable*.

The word *spy* was underlined.

Think you to hide your treachery and cowardice? I spy all. Soon others will. Your moderately tolerable life will collapse, and you will be dragged to the gallows. Crows will feast on your contemptible corpse. Did you enjoy the Reichstag's orders? A Hun like you ....

Isabella folded the letter rather than read more and returned it to the envelope before handing it back. "Why do they think you were a spy for the Germans?"

"I don't know. I am guilty of certain nefarious deeds but not of spying for the Germans."

"Were you in Germany before the war?"

"Yes. I visited my mother's family with her. She is German, but so are many of English society. Our own king changed his family's name, from Saxe-Coburg-Gotha to Windsor."

He was right. That 'shot across the bow' about the Hun would hit many of the British upper-crust. "Who knows of your mother's German heritage?"

"It's no secret."

"Who would know you committed certain nefarious deeds?"

When Richard Owen glared, those blue eyes lit with inner fire. His mouth thinned, and a muscle in his jaw jumped as he clenched and unclenched his teeth. "What are you suggesting?"

"You weren't artillery, Mr. Owen. Col. Werthy certainly wasn't, nor was he on the line. He knows many, many details, but he wasn't a trencherman. My husband was."

"Does Werthy know—?"

"I'd rather not have this discussion. The colonel and I get along perfectly swimmingly. But don't try to con me with a lie, Mr. Owen. Who on this ship would know about your war service?"

"Just Werthy. He didn't write these letters," he protested rapidly, trying to anticipate her. "He received two of them."

"Did he?" Werthy had lied to her. A spurt of anger flared up then quickly died. "I know he didn't write the letters. I think a woman did."

"A woman? How—?"

"A guess. I've no evidence. This person would have to be associated with you." *Or be very good at guessing, and no one is that good at guessing someone is a spy.* So, associated with Col. Werthy and Richard Owen, two former spies—or perhaps not former. "Who else is with you, Mr. Owen?"

"What?"

Her mind raced ahead. Former spies should recognize any man that they re-encountered, even the lowliest clerk in an office that they had merely passed through. A young or middle-aged woman would have caught their eye. Would they have noticed an older woman? "Who else is with you? You. Werthy. And who—Sheridan Ingram." She couldn't remember what Ingram younger had claimed to have done during the war.

Maybe Sheridan Ingram wasn't a spy like with Werthy. According to Nedda, his letter had charged him with adulterous deeds.

She wondered if the handwriting on Ingram's letter matched Owen's letter or her own?

Two poison pen writers?

5

When she turned to stride away, Richard Owen thrust out an arm to block her. "Mrs. Tarrant, where are you going?"

Isabella side-stepped him. "To see the colonel and Sheridan Ingram."

"You don't want to do that." His voice had darkened.

She stopped. "I don't?"

"You don't."

"Mr. Ingram's letter accused him of adultery."

"Among other nefarious deeds."

"Such as yours?"

He nodded.

"I need more answers, Mr. Owen."

"Not those answers, Mrs. Tarrant."

"Then I will speak only to the colonel. You look around, Mr. Owen, for someone you've only half-seen and not remembered. An older woman. A secretary or filing clerk. Someone who worked in an office you reported to."

As she headed to find Col. Werthy, to task him with lying to her about his letters, she realized the unknown older woman theory didn't work for accusing Mr. Owen of spying for the Germans. Why accuse him of that? What grudge might this unknown person have against him?

Did they merely want to ruin his reputation? That was bitter hatred, born of a personal grudge, a need to strike back ... because no other means of retaliation was available.

Were they trying to ruin Sheridan Ingram's reputation? Threatening him with exposure for adulterous affaires as well as being a spy. Isabella supposed more ammunition would be needed to ruin the son of a wealthy financier like Hyatt Ingram.

Richard Owen had a double accusation: spy and traitor.

What would be the second accusation against Werthy?

Then she saw a froth of white on a deck chair, white string coming from a quilted bag that held a skein of yarn, and Isabella knew she already had all the pieces she needed: an overlooked secretary of a secretive office in wartime France. A bitter mind masked by frippery talk. On this trip because she was forced from a position she must have relished. Three men from her past, either by coincidence or by plan traveling together on this Mediterranean voyage. Their future bright with potential while she had only long, disappointing years before her.

Miss Swandon's crochet hook flashed in and out.

Isabella stopped at the foot of her deck chair.

The elderly woman looked up with a beaming smile. "Mrs. Tarrant! Isn't it a wonderful day?"

She sank down on a neighboring chaise, sitting to face Miss Swandon. The quilted workbag rested on the deck between the chairs. Isabella spotted a notebook with a pencil tucked in it. She took the notebook out of the bag and idly flipped the pages, filled with writing that dashed across the pages, strong lines crossing the T's, underlining certain words.

Miss Swandon stopped her work. Her lips compressed, creating deep lines slashing down from the corners of her thin mouth. "That's private, Mrs. Tarrant. My private writing. My ideas."

"Planning your next letter, Miss Swandon?"

The crocheted square crumpled when the spinster lowered her hands to her lap. Her watery eyes shut briefly then opened to glare at Isabella. The anger wasn't as powerful as Richard Owen's, but it was there, deep and bitter, eating away like acid. "How much do you know?"

"How many letters were you planning to write?" she countered. "I suppose the last three letters would be to *The Times* in London, after you made them squirm."

"Do you know—?" She stopped, for her voice had spiraled up. When she started again, her voice was lower and hoarse, the anger under control. "Do you know what they did?"

"Nefarious deeds for their country." She used Richard Owen's words to avoid specific details. "I may not condone what they had to do, but it was war. Hopefully, it brought about the ceasefire more quickly."

"That's one thing it did," a man said.

Isabella looked around and saw Werthy at the foot of the chaise longue. Behind his shoulder stood Richard Owen.

"I won't talk to you." Miss Swandon's voice shook.

"As long as you send no more letters." Werthy perched on the deck chair's footrest. "I am saddened to hear that you are leaving the ship in Egypt, Miss Swandon." Iron hardened his voice. Isabella was glad she couldn't see his glass-clear eyes.

"My plans take me—."

"It might be better," he interrupted, voice smooth, "if you did leave then. Or have you forgotten the agreement you signed when you retired from your position with Sir George? No mention, anywhere, at any time, of anything."

The woman didn't want to answer. She bit her compressed lips. Her eyes darted around, but eventually she bowed her head. "I haven't forgotten."

"Then we know your plans, don't we?" Werthy's palm slid under Isabella's elbow and pressed upward. They stood, and he confiscated the notebook. "I will keep this. Miss Swandon, good afternoon. Mr. Owen will escort you to your cabin. I do not expect to see you again." Then he steered Isabella from the deck chairs.

She had a glimpse of Miss Swandon stuffing the crochet willy-nilly into the quilted bag, then Werthy was zooming her along the deck, past the youths at shuffleboard and the chatter of girls who cheered them on, past the young lovers mooning in the bright sunshine, past the couples strolling along the deck, and to the railing beyond the stairs to the bridge. There they stopped.

And he stared over the waters, the notebook turning and turning in his hand.

She thought he would fling it overboard, but he didn't.

When he eventually looked at her, those glass-grey eyes were hooded. "Owen said you knew we were spies."

"And you tried to deceive me. You claimed you didn't receive a letter. He said you received two." She paused, but he said nothing. She hit him with the next point that maddened her. "How many nights has Miss Swandon sat across from you at dinner? Unrecognized? Unnoticed? For a trained spy, Werthy, you are remarkably unobservant."

The shadow left his eyes. He had the gall to grin. "I was in the office only a few times, and I paid her no heed. My error. In future I will not make that mistake. We men," he added blandly, with never a cringe, "are distracted by pretty faces."

Isabella rolled her eyes and straightened away from the railing.

"Wait. How did you know?"

"I guessed." Never would she share the disparate clues she'd put together: learning crochet in France, personal secretary to an unassuming man who made deadly decisions daily, and forced into retirement after the war. There were other clues, miniscule, but hearing those three, the important three, Werthy would laugh at her. "When I saw her, watching Richard Owen, whom she shouldn't know, everything clicked." She motioned to the notebook. "What will you do with that?"

"In the wrong hands, I think this information would be dangerous. The ship has a furnace. I'll throw it in myself." He tucked it inside his jacket then withdrew his cigarette case, silver flashing in the sunlight.

With a nonchalant cast to her voice, she said, "Miss Swandon is not the person who wrote the letter to me."

Werthy winced. "No. The handwriting is different. Any ideas for your own pen pal?" He selected a thin brown cigarillo.

Isabella gave a crooked smile. "That might be fixed if you would spread your flirtations a little more widely rather than dancing every night with a young brown-eyed blonde."

"But Savina is lovely," he protested, a mock light in his eyes.

"And wealthy." She watched him strike a match before she added, "A double danger."

"Triple." Col. Werthy shook out the match then blew smoke into the wind. "I think she might be mad."

Black Heart

1

"Come to Cairo. See the pyramids," her friend Nedda had urged. "I will run mad if I have no one reasonable to talk with."

Isabella agreed with excitement. Nine days in a hotel in Port Said with nothing to do didn't appeal.

She never expected to stand on the desert road for an hour, waiting for the following truck to arrive and rescue them.

Everything around was dry desert, peaked dunes to one side of the half-burned road and ridges of mixed sienna and umber rising as a buttress against the drifting sand. Deep shadows in the ridges looked like the eyepits of a skull. The shadow-black rocks crumbled from heat and time. To her, the whole landscape looked alien, stark and intriguing.

The Egyptian desert looked nothing like Crete, where she had met her husband Madoc. The darker sandy rocks reminded her of the American southwest, where Aunt Letitia and Uncle Roger had lived, all red rock canyons or endless stretches of barren plains. Yet the desert southwest had scrubby pines, knotted junipers, and creosote bushes. Wildlife abounded: pinyon jays and wrens and thrashers, jackrabbits and coyote and deer.

Here, she only saw a distant falcon soaring on the updrafts. Nothing appeared to move in the landscape. Isabella had wanted to sketch a long-eared fennec or the precious-looking gerbil or a sleek gazelle. She'd only heard the *zit-zit-dweedle* of the scrub warbler once, as their truck jounced through the outskirts of Cairo.

Fanning herself with her wide-brimmed straw hat, she turned to watch the men standing at the road, a few yards behind the truck that had caused their halt a half-hour ago. Arms emphasizing his points, the Egyptian driver talked with Col. Werthy, Richard Owen, and Neal Gallagher. The four men had changed the first punctured tyre. It lay beside them, useless, for a tyre on the other side had also gone flat.

No one had apparently considered a second tyre blown, yet here they all stood, driver and the fifteen passengers who had crowded into the truck's cargo box. And they all watched the shimmering distance towards Cairo, hoping the second truck would arrive soon.

Nedda dropped the hand shading her eyes and turned to Isabella. She looked cool and crisp in her khaki traveling suit. Isabella, in blue cotton, felt a wrinkled lump melting in the rising heat. The ends of the green scarf tied about her dark hair fluttered in the breeze. "I'm going back into the truck before I'm burned to a crisp."

A tarp for shade was fixed above the truck box. While driving, the wind blew under the tarp and cooled them. Without movement, the dark canvas would trap the heat.

"The canopy will block the breeze," she warned.

"I can tolerate heat. I cannot stand being fried. I think my nose is burned." Nedda touched the tip gingerly.

"You should have crowded into the motorcar with the Ingrams."

Nedda rolled her eyes at the suggestion and headed for the truck.

The motorcar had paused when the truck ground to a halt. The second truck to Giza, with luggage and supplies, was supposed to be close behind, yet after a quarter-hour, it still hadn't arrived. Mr. Ingram, Nedda's employer, had given the signal to drive on. His chauffeur had consulted their truck's driver before he obeyed the order. Nedda had declined the offer to squeeze between Sheridan Ingram and the teenaged Colfax. None of the Ingrams had looked back as the Vauxhall touring car drove away.

Mrs. Gallagher and her daughter Shirley had clambered back into the truck after it was lowered from the jack. The Fremonts had joined them, complaining loudly about their discomfort. They would still be blaming the driver if Col. Werthy hadn't warned them to stop. Their daughter Savina lurked near the four men, no doubt waiting for the colonel to abandon the conversation so she could hang upon his arm.

Isabella sighed. Catching a whiff of cigarette smoke, carried from behind her, she turned to see Mrs. Phoebe Drake standing alone. Still out of the truck were four men and one woman, clustered in its shade. Only the precise Clive Rexford was unrumpled by the morning's drive. He had ridden in the cab with the driver rather than on the benches attached around the cargo box. Older than the others, he didn't slouch against the truck, unlike the two young men whose names Isabella couldn't remember.

They had pushed back their straw boaters, revealing one blond head and one ginger. Hands shoved in their jacket pockets, they scowled at the empty road.

Padgett Michaels talked with the woman he was trying to impress. Chloe Ladwick, with her soft brown curls and China blue eyes, had curves that rivaled Savina Fremont. The young men usually danced attendance on her, and Mr. Michaels appeared to have fallen into the same snare. No ingenue, she viewed her fellow passengers with jaded boredom that she didn't try to hide.

"Have you recovered from those wooden benches?" Mrs. Drake asked, coming the last few steps to stand beside Isabella. She waved her cigarette holder, lacquered red, a bit of modern chic at odds with the barren desert. "I admit to gratitude for the punctured tyres."

She smiled, sharing the sentiment. "And our hand-luggage knocking into our knees while we rattle along."

"What do you think of our fellow travelers in distress?" Although her cerulean linen dress had wrinkled, Phoebe Drake still kept her svelte poise, her dark hair in a sleek chignon and her pale skin unflushed. The widow wasn't a great beauty, but her dramatic appearance rivaled Savina and Chloe.

She judged the ten feet to the others. They chatted loudly. As she looked, Padgett Michaels passed a cigarette to the bored young woman. Lowering her voice, she said, "I wish they would not complain so loudly. We're driving across a desert. We shouldn't expect the paved roads of London."

The woman chuckled. "Is that not the behavior of the tourist abroad? To expect English roads and a green landscape, comfortable accommodations and bland food, the rain and chill of our summers? I will say that accommodations in Cairo and Port Said surprised me. Our hotel in Port Said is lovely."

"It reminds me of a house on Crete, with balcony rooms overlooking an inner garden and a fountain."

"The classic Mediterranean structure." Her bright green eyes scanned the landscape while she drew on her cigarette. The lacquered cigarette holder matched the shade of her lipstick. "I could wish our hotel in Cairo had a lovely garden."

"I believe we stay in tents at Giza. That is what Mr. Ingram told Nedda." Isabella fanned her hat.

"Tents?" Painted eyebrows lifted. Those red lips compressed, a break in her elegant mask. "We are living rough."

The conversation dried, arid as the desert. Phoebe smoked while Isabella watched the falcon soaring through the updrafts from the endless sands. The intense sunlight hurt her eyes. The heat sucked moisture from the air, refusing to let her melt.

The conversation by the road continued. Clive Rexford abandoned his group and strolled to them. The sand, shifting underfoot, prevented his usual determined stride.

At the truck, the two young men had found a point of contention. They had straightened away from the truck as they argued. One gestured, his hand cutting down. The dispute didn't yet equal the day's heat, but the Fremonts and the Gallaghers looked over the side of the truck.

Cigarette hanging from his mouth, Padget Michaels described something with minute gestures, shaping it with his hands then pointing to imaginary parts in his palm. Miss Ladwick nodded, but her gaze remained on the two men a couple of yards away.

"A pendant or a brooch?" Phoebe asked.

"I beg your pardon?"

"Our antiquities hunter. He has to be describing jewelry. Only gemstones or gold would hold Miss Ladwick's attention."

Mr. Rexford reached them. "Ladies."

"You abandoned your group just in time." Phoebe pointed with the thin red holder.

He didn't look around. "The argument would have brewed whether I stoked it or not."

Nedda had joined the watchers peering from the truck box. Her green scarf was bright against the dark tarp. Mr. Fremont called down, trying to silence the rising argument. Mr. Michaels left off his description and drew Miss Ladwick toward the rear of the truck.

Isabella looked for Werthy and Owen. They still talked to the driver although the raised voices had caught Mr. Gallagher's attention. "What is the dispute, Mr. Rexford?"

"Who knows? The heat. The dryness of the day. A wink from Miss Ladwick. Who will escort her to dinner. I have more interesting things to consider."

"Such as?" Phoebe prompted.

He scowled at the cigarette smoke wafting his way and turned to Isabella. "I find it interesting, don't you, that two tyres gave out simultaneously? Slow punctures, that's what Mr. Gallagher said. Not holes, not tears or ruptures." His precise tone clipped the words. "As if an icepick were thrust into the tyres. And here we are, stranded in the middle of the desert."

"Not quite the middle of the desert," Phoebe drawled.

"Not quite stranded," Isabella added. "The other truck will be here soon."

"Yet it is considerably delayed. I thought our driver said that we were traveling together. A curious circumstance, is it not?"

Isabella didn't want to talk about the tyres. She had avoided it with Nedda, and she didn't intend to have that conversation now. When she had a cool drink with refreshing mint, maybe then. Talking about it now only borrowed trouble.

A shout from the road drew their attention.

The driver pointed toward Cairo. Werthy and Owen shaded their eyes to peer along the road. Isabella tried to see, but the shimmering desert defeated her.

"Ah, the other truck," Rexford said.

Phoebe tossed the cigarette from the holder. "Do you see it?"

"Not yet, but what else would give our driver such joy?"

A second set of shouts came from the stopped truck. A woman screamed, brief, sharper than a raptor.

"I expected this." Rexford sounded pleased.

Beside the truck the two young men faced off, fists raised in classic boxing stance. They circled each other. They had taken the time to shed their jackets which Miss Ladwick held. She watched avidly, too avidly in Isabella's mind. *Is she the thirty that I think she is? And still acting the silly girl, impressed by boys fighting over her?*

Mr. Michaels climbed into the truck, avoiding Shirley Gallagher's escape onto the sand. Her mother's demand that she "come back this minute" added to the noise.

Col. Werthy and Richard Owen pounded past, Mr. Gallagher steps behind them. Before they arrived, a flurry of punches were thrown. Fists smacked flesh. Both men staggered back. Then they lunged forward to grapple together. One man's nose bled red onto their white shirts.

"Oh, a fight." Savina Fremont stopped beside them. "Chloe must be so pleased."

Owen grabbed one man's punching arm and forced it back.

Werthy seized the other man and flung him back. He thudded into the driver's door. Bouncing back, he met a solid punch to his jaw. That cast him back into the truck. He must have hit his head, for he slid down to the running board and slumped.

Owen held the other young man at arm's length against the side of the truck.

The shouts died. Shirley peeked around the back corner of the truck then minced over to Chloe Ladwick. The movement caught her father's attention. He rounded on her. Whatever he said, low and vehement, caused both women to exchange glances then sidle toward Isabella's group.

"He's amazing," Savina gushed. No one asked who she meant. Her attraction to the colonel was well known.

Isabella started for the truck.

Werthy whipped around. His glass-grey eyes flashed with inner fire. "Stay back. All of you. Stand over there with Rexford. The other truck is coming, and we'll have to jack this one again to change the other tyre. You two," he turned on the young men. His orders were low and curt.

They straightened and headed for the back of the truck to help the women down, one of them wiping at his bloody nose with a handkerchief.

Nedda offered him another handkerchief after he steadied her climb down. He cast the soaked one into the sand then turned to help the buxom Mrs. Fremont.

2

"Well," Nedda said when she joined Isabella, "that relieved the tedium."

The chugging diesel of the other truck heralded its steady approach. Their driver waved his arms and jumped up and down.

Dabbing at his nose, the young man stopped beside them. Except for the blood on his shirt and a cut on his cheek, he looked like any other young man, athletic and sun-touched, attractive with health. His cheerful smile seemed at odds with the fight only minutes before. Freckles dotted his face, and the wind lifted his ginger hair. He thrust the reddened handkerchief at Nedda.

"Keep it, please. I have others."

"My apologies, ladies. I shouldn't have—well." He gestured. "That will not happen again."

"See that it doesn't," Nedda said crisply, for all the world like a maiden aunt decades older rather than a few years. "We'll speak no more of it. Should you assist with the other tyre?"

"The colonel has it in hand."

The other truck rumbled and rattled in, stopping behind their truck. The driver stepped down and surveyed the problem while their driver explained. Then they two with Werthy, Owen, and Mr. Gallagher set to work. The second truck's spare replaced the second punctured tyre. The drivers rolled the discarded tyres to stow in the back of the second truck with the supplies and luggage.

Jacket over his shoulder, Werthy came to them, rolling down the sleeves of his shirt. His eyes had lost their lightning ferocity. The wind ruffled his dark hair, grown longer in the three weeks that Isabella had known him. Behind him, Owen herded the other passengers to the first truck. "I want you two riding in the cab with me. Owen will drive the other truck."

"What?" Nedda protested, but Isabella merely nodded. "First truck or second?"

"Second. Owen will drive the first one. He'll take Caveley in the cab with him. Hetteridge can ride in cargo with both drivers, in with the luggage. I think it wise that we keep them separated for the rest of the drive."

"Why were they fighting?"

He shrugged into his jacket. "Caveley said that Hetteridge hit him for no reason."

"They were arguing," Nedda pointed out. "They had a reason."

"You were there. What did you hear?"

"Nothing that made sense."

"Then we'll find out at camp, when we've all had time to cool down."

"Are we far from camp?" Isabella asked, wishing this day and its fraught events laid to rest. The sun rode high in the sky. Hours would have to pass before her wish came true.

"Another half-hour, Khalil says. Over the next rise we should see the pyramids. You'll have time for photographs with the great Sphinx and to walk around. Try a few sketches," he added, knowing Isabella had her sketchbook.

He searched out his cigarette case and matches.

"And take yet more dictation from Mr. Ingram." Nedda sighed heavily.

Lighting his cigarillo, Werthy paused long enough to give a broad grin. When the thin cigar was going, he nodded to the second truck. "I'm driving. Get your things and put them in the cab."

Even enclosed and cramped with three on the seat, the truck cab was more comfortable than the wooden benches in the cargo box. The wind gusted through the open windows and swirled around. The pyramids soon appeared in the cracked windshield, dominant but hazy in the midday heat. The nine pyramids filled the sandy plain, called the Giza Necropolis. The tallest loomed over the others. They didn't look like any other structure Isabella had seen. They were alien as the arid desert, intriguing in their difference.

Dust streamed away from the wheels of the truck ahead. The canopy flopped, admitting flashes of light into the cargo box. The others jounced on the wooden benches, fixed around the two sides and against the cab's back. With Werthy's rearrangement, they were less crowded. Talkative Shirley Gallagher squeezed between her parents. Savina and Chloe chatted. Mr. Fremont had his arms folded, not talking to his wife, who dabbed her brow and neck with a white handkerchief. Rexford and Michaels sat across from each other, also not talking.

Nedda drew the green scarf from her dark head. "Tell us, colonel, the reason you wanted a private conversation before we reached camp."

He glanced over then directed his gaze to the sand-sifted road. "It's what the other driver told us while we changed the tyre."

"About this delay?"

"He had to change trucks. The first one refused to run. He drove it with no trouble this morning, all the way from the garage to the hotel, but the motor sputtered then quit before he managed fifty feet from the hotel. Sand in the petro tank."

"Sand? How does—?" Isabella stopped.

"Sabotage," he answered. "While this truck had two punctured tyres. Owen thought an icepick."

"Mr. Rexford told us that. Mr. Gallagher told him."

"Sabotage," Nedda mused. "With an icepick from the hotel? And sand from the streets. Easy enough, I suppose. It's simply another prank. Like the latches that broke on Miss Harlow's suitcase. Every dock worker had a view of her unmentionables."

"She was mortified." Isabella remembered the older woman's profuse apologies and tears. "We think she was targeted because she was a missionary."

"Harmless pranks," Nedda added. "Like the fountain pen exploding all over that girl's dimity dress in the Reading Salon."

"And salt switched for sugar when the hotel served breakfast before we left Cairo."

"The deck chairs that came unscrewed. Colfax told his grandfather about that. It's the one time that young man exhibited any interest in what happened aboard ship."

"I saw him around the trucks this morning," Isabella quietly inserted, "while we gathered."

Werthy ground his teeth. "That's not good. Sherry assured me the boy wouldn't be a problem."

"For your secret mission?"

He leaned forward to glare around Isabella at Nedda. "Just what do you know, Miss Cortland?"

"Isabella shared an interesting bit of information about you and Richard Owen and Sheridan Ingram."

"Nedda! You had already guessed!" she protested.

"How much do you know, Miss Cortland?"

"A better question would ask what I don't know," she drawled, "but we shan't speak of that. Better to talk about all of those shipboard pranks." Her dark eyes opened wide as she looked at Isabella. She nudged with her elbow. "Like gluing the discs to the shuffleboard deck."

"And the marbles that escaped from the basket of dinner rolls and rolled around the dining room. That poor steward's face."

"The pranks aren't so harmless," he retorted. "Milton Tavistock broke a leg falling down the stairs yesterday morning. His wife nearly fell as well, hurrying to reach him. A wire was stretched across the stair."

"Poor Mr. Tavistock. I wondered the reason he and his wife didn't come on this excursion. I thought they had changed to go to Alexandria. I didn't hear about his fall."

"Nor I," Nedda said. "Nor did I know about the salt and sugar."

Isabella patted her friend's knee. "Not all the salt cellars and sugar bowls were switched. You left early, remember? Mr. Ingram had a telegram to send."

"But the switched salt and sugar and the tyres means the prankster came on this excursion. He didn't stay on the *Nomadic* or in Port Said. He's with us."

"Or she," Werthy inserted.

The camp came into view through the cracked windshield. The Giza Necropolis was an active archaeological site. The diggings were a busy hive, with tarps placed near the excavations, reminding Isabella of the dig on Crete. Cold dread worked down her spine and prickled the hair on her arms.

Beyond the diggings were the tents, the largest for gathering places like the dining tent and the kitchen. Behind those, with the Sphinx and the largest pyramid as backdrops, were smaller tents, more than a dozen, their sleeping quarters.

She stared at the people riding in the back of the first truck. Strangers, all of them, although she knew their names. *Who is the prankster?*

Workers swarmed over the diggings. Others stood at the base of a small pyramid. Three people climbed it. They were scorpions, arms stretched wide as they reached for the next stone.

"I count over a dozen malicious pranks," Werthy said, shifting gears as the trucks followed a curving road into the camp. "Be careful. We're staying in tents. Those are open to anyone. Double-check it, your cots, your suitcases, especially if the tent has been vacant for a long while. Eat and drink only what everyone else does. If you alone are served a dish, don't take it."

"That's rude to any host," Nedda argued. "Mr. Ingram said a local sheikh will host us tonight. We must take anything offered."

"Then don't eat if other people don't receive it."

"Pretend to taste it," she countered. "Do not offend our host."

Isabella nodded, but "Do you think we're targets? How could we be?"

"You two shared that balcony stair with the Tavistocks," he said, and another shiver trembled through her.

"I would think our prankster doesn't care who's hurt by his mischief."

"A youth? They like pranks. Are you thinking of Colfax, Nedda?"

She shrugged. "Or a teen-aged girl, like Shirley Gallagher. Have you watched her interaction with her mother? Nothing but criticisms. Or a young man, unhappy with his world, like that Thomas Hetteridge throwing the first punch."

"Or Michael Caveley himself." Isabella had finally remembered his whole name.

"Better to list who it can't be." He shifted gears. The truck slowed as it headed into the camp propre.

3

By sunset, the smell of roasting lamb filled the air.

The local sheikh had a dramatic entrance on a camel. Everyone stopped their preparations for the evening to watch his ride into camp, with six escorts. The camels lowered, front down then rear, and the men dismounted, white-robed with the typical patterned headscarf. Each had a military rifle strapped across his chest, a strange juxtaposition of the old world with the modern one.

The archaeologist in charge of the diggings, Dr. Brunsen greeted the sheikh. They talked briefly before he brought him to meet Hyatt Ingram and his son. Three of the white-robed guards followed, ducking into one of the larger tents behind the men.

Dinner that evening with the sheikh was eye-opening because the women didn't dine with him, only the men.

The men gathered around low tables on pillows. Ornate rugs covered the floor. Brass lanterns hung from a rope down the tent's center. Isabella had managed a peek inside before the women were shuffled off to a smaller tent with a dinner table. Two candelabra provided light. Their chairs were backless camp stools. The china had seen better years. Tarnish stained the fork tines and the beading around the handles. When Mrs. Fremont complained of tea rather than wine, she was shushed by Mrs. Brunsen. "Our host is a devout Muslim. No alcoholic beverages are permitted."

Yet service was prompt, with two women bringing basins and towels to wash their hands. A girl with a pipe softly played a melodic tune.

Mrs. Brunsen detailed the morrow for them. The more adventurous would have a camel ride around the whole necropolis. Others could tour one of the lesser pyramids. Isabella was disappointed to hear that the pyramids predated any hieroglyphics or artwork.

The entrée was grilled lamb, *kafta*. Isabella and Nedda enjoyed the spicy oil served with it and dipped in pieces of bland pita-style bread. Savina, Chloe, and Shirley protested the green mash *besarah*. According to Mrs. Bronsen, the honey balls served with dates and walnuts were Cleopatra's favorite dessert. The young women gobbled up the sweet and asked for more. Then Nedda muttered, "A sweet tooth is 'immortal longing'. We need only robe and crown." With that reference to Shakespeare's *Antony and Cleopatra*, Isabella had to hide her giggle behind her napkin.

They had no reason to linger over dinner. Lighting their lanterns, they left the tent. A tenor's high notes soared into the night from the other tent, and somewhere in the darkness a fennec's high-pitched bark pierced through the song. Lantern lights bobbed about as they stumbled over rocks and veered off then onto the barely-visible path.

Then Mrs. Gallagher turned her ankle and fell. She tried to make light of her fall with "these curséd heels", but her ankle swelled rapidly. Nedda pulled her up, and Isabella helped bolster her hobble to her tent. Shirley led the way with both lanterns. The woman sighed with relief when they lowered her to the cot. "This day has had nothing but trouble."

"That ankle needs a compress," Nedda judged. "I think the dig has a doctor."

"Mrs. Brunsen will know. She hasn't left the dining tent. Shirley, run to tell her, please."

While they waited, they puttered a bit, taking off Mrs. Gallagher's shoes and stockings and wetting a towel to lay over the swelling. They lit the large tent lantern and poured a sip of Mr. Gallagher's whiskey, stored in a flask tucked in his valise, and coaxed the woman to drink it.

Shirley dashed back, errand done and out of breath, as Isabella screwed the cap on the flask. "Mrs. Brunsen will tell him. He's with the men."

The singing broke off, leaving only the intermittent bark of the desert fox. The animal had found a friend who answered from across the plain. When Mr. Gallagher shouldered into the tent, a thin man in a loose jacket behind him, they crowded to one side then stole away.

The men's dinner had broken up. Several robed men stood outside the large tent. Others in trousers walked around, some heading for the tents, others going toward the archaeologists' tents near the excavation.

"That was no prank, just a simple accident," Nedda murmured as they reached their tent. She held the lantern aloft as Isabella untied the tent flaps then ducked inside. "I'll be glad when this day is over."

Isabella started in, then Nedda shrieked and stumbled back, knocking her out of the tent. She nearly fell, her balance upset again when Nedda bumped into her as she scrambled out of the tent.

"Get back. Oh, get back," she gasped. "Snake. Snake. Snake!" she screamed the third time.

Isabella towed her away from the tent. "What? Where?"

"In the—in the—."

A man muscled past. "Stay back." Werthy held a pistol aloft. "Where is it?"

"In the tent."

"On the floor," Nedda clarified.

"Give me your lantern."

Nedda handed it over. The light shook and shuddered then steadied when he took it.

Another man ran up. Richard Owen, his jacket off but a pistol in his hand and a torch in the other. "Hold the tent flap open," Werthy ordered. "Stay out of my line of fire."

With the flap drawn back, Isabella saw a dark rope on the tent floor. It moved. Werthy fired. Then he stepped in, blocking her view. Owen dropped the tent flap as he also ducked inside.

Isabella gave Nedda a shake. "Were you bitten? Were you bitten?"

"I think I'm going to be sick." She gulped.

"No, you aren't. You are the unflappable and efficient secretary. Nothing bothers you."

"I wish. It's all an act," but her voice had steadied.

Owen emerged, the lantern-light burnishing his hair to gold. Werthy came out, holding a three-foot length of brown rope that had once lived and slithered.

Isabella didn't want to know but asked anyway. "What is it?"

"African egg snake. Not venomous."

"How did—? I don't like snakes," Nedda said faintly and began to shiver again.

"There's a basket on your floor with the lid half-off."

"A basket?" The women exchanged a look. "We didn't have a basket. And we're definitely not having any dealings with snakes."

"No." Werthy's eyes glinted, reflecting the amber light. "Our prankster strikes again." His mouth set in a grim line. Owen, younger, was no less angry.

The others crowded around, eager to hear what had happened. Isabella leaned her head against Nedda's shoulder and wished she had stayed in dull Port Said with nothing to do. The *Nomadic* would be restocked with coal and resupplied and on its way back around the Mediterranean. Her new friend Lady Peverell had remained on it, starting her voyage home. The next ship, a sailing barque, would arrive in less than a week. It would take them through the Suez Canal and to the next ship, the *Garipoola*. Boredom looked quite safe.

"Would you check our tent again? To be certain."

Werthy handed the remains of the snake to the Egyptian who had run up with the others, clamoring to know what had happened.

Isabella spotted a couple of the sheikh's guards standing at the back of the crowd.

While the colonel ducked inside the tent, Owen answered a dozen questions before he ordered them away. "Excitement's over. It's late, and we start early tomorrow. Get some sleep." When some protested, he jutted that square jaw. "Enough. Head to your tents. You can ask your questions tomorrow."

Tent cleared, Isabella still was reluctant to venture inside.

"You ladies can have my tent," Owen offered.

"No. No, it's clear. The colonel said it was." Isabella looked down, hiding her blinking eyes. "Thank you, Emerson."

He gripped her shoulder, squeezing hard. "I'm near. Owen is in with me."

She nodded then turned to the tent.

Neither she nor Nedda slept a wink.

4

They rose before sunrise to wash and dress. Three cups of dark coffee had Isabella wired but no less tired.

"What now?" Nedda asked. "Do you think someone will drive us back to Cairo?"

"The hotel doesn't expect us until tomorrow."

"The next prank might be deadly."

"They've only been malicious thus far."

"You heard what the colonel said. Milton Tavistock has a broken leg. It could easily have been a broken neck."

Her friend was right. Werthy had been right to warn them. And the tyres could have burst, wrecking the truck and tossing them around like fragile sticks. "What do you think about these pranks?"

"Malicious, like you said."

"But not designed to hurt. It's as if the prankster isn't thinking about consequences."

"To himself? Or herself?"

"No. He—or she—doesn't expect to be caught, but he's also not considering the consequences to his victims. Only his enjoyment of setting up the prank and seeing what happens."

"Like a malicious child."

"Is Colfax malicious, Nedda? I know you don't interact with him, but—."

After a sip of strong coffee, Nedda tilted back her head and stared at the hazy sun climbing the ladder of clouds on the horizon. "He's bored. There's little for him to do. He was looking forward to the camel ride. He could care less about a pile of blocks or a misshapen stone face in the desert."

"He had things to do aboard ship. The gymnasium. Shuffleboard. There were youths his age. And no tutor or boring lessons. Wasn't he glad to have freedom? I thought I saw him reading a massive tome on deck."

"Trautwine. *The Civil Engineer's Pocket-book*. He wants to be an engineer, which disappoints his grandfather. I wouldn't call the boy malicious. Bored, certainly. What was it you said days ago? *Idle hands are the devil's workshop.* He does think ahead. Colfax is remarkably foresighted for a teenager. He would consider the consequences of pranks to people." The last destroyed all of Isabella's suspicions, then Nedda added, "Whether he would *enjoy* considering those consequences, I do not know."

"Would you call Shirley Gallagher malicious?"

"That girl craves excitement, but I don't see her keeping a snake in a basket. Would she be off the parental leash long enough to find a snake?"

"Not her."

"Not Clive Rexford either."

"I don't know." Isabella pondered. "I think he's secretly laughing at us."

"Oh, most definitely, but these pranks are too messy for that tidy man."

"Who then? Padgett Michaels or Michael Caveley? Phoebe Drake or Chloe Ladwick? I think we can rule out the Gallaghers and the Fremonts."

"But not Savina Fremont."

"No. Except for the snake."

"Then that rules out Chloe Ladwick," Nedda countered.

"I don't know. I can see her planning the pranks and buying the snake then getting Caveley or Hetteridge to carry it for her. But I didn't see any basket in the luggage, did you? Could the snake have been bought here?"

"And we're back to square one." She sighed dramatically. "We didn't mention the Ingrams elder and younger or Richard Owen or Emerson Werthy."

"Seriously?"

"Seriously, Isabella. I suppose we're going to tempt fate with a tour of the pyramid."

"I suppose we are."

The morning advanced. The sun had climbed above the cloud ladder and glared across the desert plain before the others emerged.

Mrs. Gallagher kept to her tent. Hyatt Ingram did as well.

Breakfast was subdued. The dining tent, its sides raised to admit fresh air, had another table and more camp stools. Coffee, eggs, and more of the bland pita bread was offered. Mr. Fremont demanded "What else?" The servants gave him a blank stare before continuing with their work.

Then Mr. Gallagher and his daughter, the Fremont parents, Phoebe Drake, Padgett Michaels, and Sheridan and Colfax Ingram were herded together for the camel tour.

Escorted by one of Dr. Brunsen's students, the rest of them headed for one of the lesser pyramids.

Nedda and Isabella walked together. Isabella had tucked a thermos with water in with her sketchbook in a tote. She had found a walking stick and vowed not to lose it. Nedda had an officer's field bag, the strap crossing her breast. She kept a hand on it until they began the climb to the pyramid's entrance, fifty yards or so from the base.

Savina demanded Werthy's assistance while Hetteridge and Caveley jockeyed for who would help Chloe. Rexford claimed he would climb to the top and kept going past the entrance. The sole Egyptian with them stayed with the older man, occasionally hauling him up to the next block. Owen kept up with the student, looking back to see if anyone wanted help before climbing higher.

The student, lantern in hand, ducked first into the passageway. He had warned them about the sloping corridor, but he hadn't mentioned how narrow it was. By the time they reached the Queen's Chamber, Isabella's heart raced and her breath came faster. *Claustrophobia*, she told herself, but that didn't help the unnatural fear. The flickering lights ahead and behind did nothing to help.

"The King's Chamber is at the end of this passageway." The student bounded ahead.

Chloe gazed at the ascending gallery. "I'm tired. I'll wait here."

"I'll stay with you," Hetteridge declared, and Nedda gave Isabella a sidelong glance. "Owen, give us your lantern. We'll wait for you to come back."

He handed it over. "Anyone else staying?"

Isabella considered it—*but what if I'm wrong?* If the prankster was Chloe Ladwick, what could she do? The entrance couldn't be blocked; there was no door to shut. Although littered with rubble, the gallery was straight. No side passage would confuse them.

Even if Hetteridge was Chloe's accomplice, what could they do?

Caveley already walked the narrow gallery, following the student archaeologist.

Werthy glanced at Isabella. She determinedly started forward, Nedda behind her.

The climb to the King's Chamber took forever. The air grew hotter and stuffier, so close it was hard to breathe. Isabella kept her focus on the lantern ahead, still ascending. Werthy held the other lantern, and she knew he wouldn't let it go. Rocky debris littered the gallery, and she watched each step, using her stick as balance. Savina's complaints began long before the student's lantern-light faded. Isabella's heart jumped, then she realized he had entered the upper chamber.

Caveley exclaimed, but the faint light ahead remained. Werthy's lantern flickered more as the air grew stale, but progress remained steady.

The King's Chamber was bare, looted long ago, the sarcophagus removed by the first archaeologists who explored the great tomb. A few wooden supports lay on the floor, not needed and therefore abandoned, never removed.

Caveley held the student's lantern aloft, directing the light into a narrow shaft.

"Granite," the student said. "There's small rooms above here. We're still speculating on the purpose. Treasure chambers? Secondary burials of worthy concubines? Sacrifices to ensure the pharoah's passage to the afterlife? Some kind of support system? We've had an engineer in, but he wouldn't give a definitive answer."

"And this shaft?"

"Another mystery. Maybe for ventilation? Or a religious ceremony that admits the sunlight of the great god Ra? And look at this, scratched into the stone here." He smoothed his hand over the wall opposite the entrance. The waist-height etching was barely visible. "I think this is an attempt at an ankh, the key of life. Dr. Brunsen disagrees. He thinks a looter scratched it into the stone. The first archaeologists did find skeletons in here, wearing garb that was certainly not of ancient Egypt."

"A looter who became trapped and died?" Caveley swung his lantern. "How many skeletons? Col. Werthy, bring your lantern over. We might see it better. Mrs. Tarrant, come away from the entrance. You have to see this."

Isabella didn't move.

"I believe the record says six skeletons were found."

"Ha. There's six of you. See it? Scratched in here. Huh. Maybe two lanterns are too many. I can hardly see it now." Caveley retreated from the wall.

"It does depend on a lesser amount of light," the student said, ever helpful.

Savina bent to peer into the blocked shaft. "This was used for ceremonies to a sun god?"

"Here, Owen, take a look. I'll back out of the way," Caveley offered.

Then Owen stumbled into Werthy. The lantern swayed. He righted himself. "You oaf! Caveley, get back from me!"

Instead, the young man shoved again, hard. Owen staggered into the colonel. That thrust Werthy against the wall.

And his lantern went out.

Even as the men regained their balance, Caveley leaped away. A metallic clink and snip, and the King's Chamber plunged into darkness.

Savina screamed then began weeping.

The distant light from the Queen's Chamber barely reached them.

Isabella saw a shadow rush to her and swiped with her stick, hoping to trip him, but it was too late. Caveley ran into the gallery, starting his descent toward the only other light, held by Hetteridge in the far-away Queen's Chamber. His laughter echoed back, raucous and harsh.

"Well," said Nedda dryly, "that was totally expected." She flicked on a torch. "All three of them, do you think?"

Isabella peered down the long gallery. A figure ran down the narrow passage, straight and true to the other light. "Shall we ask?"

"You knew? And said nothing?" Werthy sounded angrier than she'd ever heard him. In the stark shadows cast by the torch, he was a grim mask heralding doom.

"We suspected a prank, not who was the prankster."

"All speculation and nothing provable. Until now." Nedda shined her torch down the gallery. "Who's first?"

Werthy pushed past and headed down, Owen steps behind him, another vengeful incarnation of doom. Nedda followed.

"If you'll help Savina," Isabella told the student. "I think we better move fast."

5

They caught up to the three pranksters at the tents.

Isabella missed the first part of the altercation. She arrived as Werthy punched Caveley. The young man plowed in and received rapid jabs to his gut, another bloodied nose, and a last punch that knocked him back and to the ground.

"Here now!" Hetteridge planted himself beside Chloe. "We didn't do anything wrong. No one is hurt."

"Tell that to Milton Tavistock," Owen said. The sun-bronzed demigod knocked Hetteridge in the jaw. The young man's head tipped back, then he dropped and didn't move.

"Tommy! Tommy! Look what you've done!" Chloe dropped to her knees and tried to lift his head from the dirt.

"What if that snake had been venomous?" Werthy demanded.

"The man in the bazaar said it wasn't! Besides, I'm not talking to you. You're a barbarian! Tommy, open your eyes. Tommy, I need you!"

"What if the truck had overturned when the tyres went?"

"But it didn't. Tommy! Michael, *do* something."

On one elbow, Caveley surveyed Werthy, fists at his side, eyes like lightning. He rubbed his jaw. "Game's over, I guess."

For several anxious moments, Isabella feared Werthy would rip him from the ground and deliver more punishment. Then he whirled and stalked away. She hied after, Nedda with her, and Owen striding behind.

The day wasn't a total loss. The camel tour was a great success, and Colfax Ingram amused them at dinner by recounting the ride.

Someone collapsed the tent on Hetteridge and Caveley during the night.

And someone ensured the three pranksters had no breakfast.

Hyatt Ingram informed them that they would have to find their own way to Cairo. The trucks he'd hired wouldn't take them.

When the three arrived in the capitol, dusty and tired, shadows black under their eyes, their hotel reservations had been cancelled.

That happened in Port Said, too.

The passenger steamer for the canal could find no evidence of their bookings. The pranksters didn't reach Jeddah in time to board the *Garipoola*.

Savina called Col. Werthy "my hero". When Isabella deemed his temper had cooled, she and Nedda did as well.

Silver Web

1

Lightning forked across the sky, piercing white and bright across the drenched skylight of the lounge. Thunder cracked overhead, drowning the faint shouts of sailors at their stations. Rain deluged the slick decks and flooded the windows. The *Garipoola* plunged down a billowing wave then canted over as another wave struck the ship broadside. Passengers screamed as they clung to the bolted-down settees and tables in the lounge.

Isabella cast a prayer heavenward and wished she were in her cabin with fewer objects to fly her way. The storm had struck the ship an hour before. The steward reassured them it was little more than a rain event. As the clock ticked through the hour, the storm intensified until the steward fled the lounge to seek refuge elsewhere.

The ship righted. Water sluiced over the glassed ceiling. The rain fell, a deluge that dimmed the day to twilight.

With Isabella on the bolted-down settee were the Australia-bound Reynolds family, the three children clustered at their parents' feet. The youngest, the only daughter, crowded between her father's long legs, clinging to his shins. The two boys crouched before their mother and Isabella. They had turned two chairs onto their sides as a barrier against other sliding chairs. On the floor beside her were Sheridan and Colfax Ingram, the father with an arm around his son's shoulders. They braced against the wall and had hooked two chairs together as defense

The elder Ingram had never reached the lounge. He had remained in his cabin, examining accounts with his secretary Nedda Cortland. The Ingrams and their retinue, secretary and servants, would leave when the ship docked in Muscat. Already, Isabella mourned the loss of her friend Nedda.

Her other friend, Col. Werthy was also absent from the lounge. Like Isabella, he and his protégé Richard Owen were bound for India. They would debark in Bombay while she traveled on to Madras. She had no idea where Werthy had found sanctuary from the storm.

Tie askew and hair mussed, Clive Rexford sat beyond the Ingrams, and beyond him was the mutton-chopped Nelson Fullerton, also bound for India. The Fremonts, parents and daughter Savina, crowded on one side of the banquette fastened to the outer wall. Sharing the other side were the missionary Miss Harlow and a couple that Isabella barely knew, the Rathburns.

Another wave struck the *Garipoola*. Women screamed. Men cursed. Lightning flashed, a penetrating brilliance that illuminated the skylight and the windows along the lounge walls. Then the ship struggled up another surging wave. Unsecured chairs, broken fragments of china, books, and bags slid across the floor. Rain spattered the glass, pinging like hailstones.

A shadow passed along the windows, braving the wave-assaulted deck. A sailor, struggling to a different station as the ship fought the storm. He plastered against the windows, a distorted blur soaked by seawater, arms upraised as he clung to the window bracing, dark hair plastered to his head. His face looked very white against the glass.

A wave splashed the windows. When the water washed off the glass, the sailor had reached the end of the bank of windows, behind the Fremonts. The ship pitched starboard, throwing him against the glass again. Then he levered himself past the window and out of sight.

She couldn't see the people clustered along the aft wall of the lounge. The Gallagher family had one of the corner banquettes on starboard while Phoebe Drake and Edwina Bridgewater clung to Richard Owen on the window-side of the banquette.

Padgett Michaels sat beside the door, making a feeble attempt to avoid the water puddling at the threshold. On the door's other side were Edgar Lear and another young man, bound for India. The elderly Lady Bernhardt and the Saunders crowded onto the settee opposite hers. Then came more people that Isabella didn't know, some who had joined them at Jeddah when they all transferred to the *Garipoola*. Mr. Collins seemed very much a London barrister. Robin Kennedy was bound for Australia, like the Reynolds. Allan Gregory would stop in India before heading on to China, like the Fremonts.

Sheltering in the final corner banquette were the Titus Malcolms, the Winston Tuchmans, a middle-aged manager returning to his rubber plantation, and Dr. Bauer, the ship's doctor. The doctor on the *Nomadic* had kept to his miniature hospital with its full complement of medical staff for its thousand passengers. The *Garipoola* was much smaller and older than the queen of the British-Asia Oceanic line, and Dr. Bauer often mingled with them.

She wondered how the passengers fared who had retreated to their cabins at the first signs of the storm.

As the *Garipoola* bucked and plunged, Isabella wished she were back on the larger *Nomadic*. Capt. Locke had the weathered features of a man long at sea. She didn't doubt his experience, but this storm would tax the greatest captain's abilities. She dipped her head to her hands, clinging to the settee's arm, and prayed God would calm this raging sea.

An eternity later, the lightning lost its brilliance. Waves no longer breached the ship decks. Thunder rumbled distantly. Rain pattered gently against the glass. The ship sliced easily through the waves. Twilight came, the light unchanged but the clock announcing day's end.

The steward reappeared to announce dinner in a half-hour. "A freak storm," he answered the clamoring questions and claimed the night sky of the Arabian Sea was an unmatched marvel.

When she went to dress for dinner, Isabella found little disturbed in her cabin, a single berth with a tiny alleyway between the bunk and the cabinet wall. She picked up a pen that rolled on the floor then slipped into a simple frock. The air in her little lavatory was humid, curling her hair around her face.

She encountered Nedda on the deck near the dining room's entrance. The secretary had a single berth much like Isabella's although nearer to the stateroom of her employer. "I see you survived the storm."

Nedda rolled her eyes. "You look none the worse. Were you in your cabin?"

"No. The lounge. It was horrid."

"Did you worry that the glass would break? Especially the ceiling."

"I didn't even think of that!"

"Lucky you. Mr. Ingram discovered seasickness."

"You poor thing!" for she knew that Nedda would have had to deal with any of her employer's problems. Hyatt Ingram never talked business around his valet.

"One benefit: he won't join us tonight."

Then they were in the dining room, slowly filling up even though the half-hour had passed. They plastered on their company smiles as they slid into their chairs at the Ingrams' table. Colfax Ingram was also absent although Sheridan Ingram was there, serving as host in his father's stead.

Emerson Werthy and Richard Owen had the other chairs. "And where did you ride out the storm?" Isabella asked. "Mr. Owen was in the lounge with us, keeping the Mesdames Drake and Bridgewater from sliding to the floor."

"In the pilothouse with the captain." Throughout dinner, he regaled them with Capt. Locke's stoicism and the pilot's jittery nerves.

Tonight's quick soup revealed the chef's own worries during the storm. Rice curry with chicken followed, a simple dish that hid its quick preparation with spices. The usual third course was nonexistent. Irish coffee and hot cocoa were offered.

The older passengers retired early, but the storm had left many restless and edgy. Usually after dinner, Isabella improved her bridge game with Mr. Rexford, Mr. Fullerton, and whoever would make the fourth. Mr. Fullerton cried off.

"There's dancing." Mr. Rexford surprised her with the offer and steered her to the long room known as the saloon at night and the lounge during the day.

2

Tinny dance music swelled onto the decks through opened windows. The saloon lights looked bright, with a kaleidoscope of shifting colors. When the music wound down, the colors stopped and became dancers waiting for the next song. Voices replaced the music until the gramophone started up and the carousel of colors resumed.

Isabella on his arm, Mr. Rexford paused on the threshold. The room sorted into dancing couples, men standing or sitting along the walls, to which the tables and chairs were removed. A bar had opened at the far end, and a steward maneuvered a tray among the spectators.

The saloon looked nothing like the daytime lounge.

"You know this song?" Mr. Rexford swung her into a foxtrot that matched the jazzy music.

His agility surprised her. She knew he was a fixture in London society, but she'd never associated him with dancing. Ever precise, he didn't talk as they danced but looked around. That inattention gave Isabella permission to look as well.

She spotted Phoebe Drake and Savina Fremont and Edwina Bridgewater, the Gallaghers and the Reynolds, the Tuchmans and the Malcolms.

When the music ended, Mr. Rexford stepped back . . . and Padgett Michaels appeared. "You permit?" Aware that the next song had started, she managed to nod. Partnered couples were changing, men leaving the floor as other men replaced them.

Mr. Michaels started with a basic foxtrot.

The saloon had a strange energy. It reminded her of a coiled rattlesnake, shaking its rattle and ready to strike.

Mr. Michaels kept her successfully diverted. "Good of you to join us. Mrs. Tarrant. You'll be in high demand."

"You need more women," for the ship had a serious dearth of women passengers. "Is the saloon always this crowded?"

"Not usually. The storm, you know. Can you spin?" and he surprised her with one.

By the third spin, she added a sashay to her whirl that brought a smile to his dour face.

The dance gave her a new view of Padgett Michaels. She'd considered him stodgy, conversing only about the exotic jewelry and antiquities he found in the Middle East. She never expected a dancer who enjoyed spins and dips.

Her next partner, Lionel Wexford, provided a reason for the saloon's vibrating energy that looked for a victim. "You heard? We've a thief among us." He sniffed. "Bad form. The thief must be extremely clever to take his pick of the jewels aboard."

"A thief? Whatever do you mean?"

"The thief broke into Lady Bernhardt's cabin during the storm. That silver necklace she wears every evening, he stole it."

"That beautiful necklace? It was stolen?"

"An expensive piece." His arm tightened on her waist which was his signal for a series of sliding moves for his version of a one-step dance. "Even broken up by the fence, the diamonds will bring a pretty price."

"How horrible. That's the reason Lady Bernhardt didn't come to dinner."

"I assume our good captain was with her, promising to find the thief, I'm certain. He will have to work fast. We dock tomorrow night. Our thief will escape then."

"I cannot believe it. Stolen! Who could the thief be?"

He shrugged and turned her. "Apparently, all the stewards are accounted for during the storm, so one of the passengers must be the culprit."

"She loved that necklace." Isabella mourned for Lady Bernhardt.

The elegant necklace, all diamonds and white-gold, started as a single braided strand around the neck before dividing into three separate strands over the upper bodice. Two caret-sized diamonds framed the front design, a display of loops upon loops, each loop attached to the white-gold chains with smaller diamonds. The showpiece was a teardrop diamond pendant surrounded with glittering emeralds.

Isabella's first glimpse of the necklace was the evening they left Jeddah. It had taken her breath away, and every sighting since had confirmed the glory of the necklace.

She danced fourth with Mr. Reynolds, who kept to a simple box-step. He talked of the theft for a bit. Then he started a running commentary about his family's immigration to Australia. "My uncle runs sheep, you know."

Edgar Lear elbowed in for the next dance. She considered refusing him, but Sheridan Ingram didn't look upset to have lost his chance to dance.

Mr. Lear didn't want to talk about the theft. He mumbled that the necklace was probably insured then talked about the ferocity of the storm. He missed a few steps, hurting her toes, and kept looking around the room.

The gramophone wound down before the song ended. Isabella escaped with "I must sit. You've exhausted me."

"This is the last but next song," he complained.

"I simply must sit. I'm not as athletic as you are, Mr. Lear."

His brow furrowed. A muscle twitched in his jaw, but he led her to some chairs and demanded a man give up his seat to her.

She didn't know anyone clustered around the chairs. Mr. Lear abandoned her before the re-wound song came to an end. The men asked her to dance. Isabella let the clamor wash over her while she tried to think of a polite refusal. Then the starting music became a tango. The clamor died.

A firm hand cupped her elbow, urging her from the chair. "You know the tango?"

Isabella looked into Emerson Werthy's cool-ice eyes. "I do."

Within minutes, she knew she had volunteered for trouble. Werthy was the ideal partner, assured and masterful, and the tango was a dance for lovers. Her husband Madoc had taught her to dance in close embrace, and Werthy had the same style. She kept flashing to Madoc as she followed Werthy's lead.

More than trouble, for her awareness of him as an attractive man entwined with her perception of him as a close friend.

The repetitive pulse of the music took over the beat of her heart. He kept his hand high on her back, embracing her closely when the music became dramatic. In the *rueda,* he turned her so her heart crossed into his. She broke apart for the swing out, and he drew her back with a snap that brought her in close contact with his lean body.

Isabella stumbled once, as they stepped in and around each other, the tangle of steps of the *ocho* that symbolically entwined them. He kept her close, her cheek against his chin, his breath wafting the curls around her face, the heat of his body like a furnace against her. He swung her to the right then pivoted her twice. As the music ended, he rocked her back then forward, into him, tangled with him.

The music didn't resume. Chatter started up and swelled in volume. Someone shoved a wine glass into her hand. Werthy, she realized. "Drink," he muttered, "you look too pale." He glanced away to speak to Sheridan Ingram.

She sipped the wine, a fruity white that was too sweet. *He knows*, and color burned her cheeks. She veered her gaze away from his broad shoulders to the golden-curled beauty gazing up at him. Savina Fremont. Her bright red lipstick looked a garish slash across her face.

Then Isabella's eyes narrowed and fastened on the pearl eardrop missing from her left ear. "Savina, you've lost an earring."

"What?" Her hand flew to her ears. "Oh no! It's gone!" The topaz at the top of the right eardrop twinkled.

"It must have fallen off," a man said. Clive Rexford, appearing suddenly, for she'd not seen him for almost an hour.

"It wouldn't just fall off," Isabella countered. "It's a screwback. Isn't it, Savina?"

"It would have had to fall off," Robin Kennedy said. He'd escorted Savina to their little group and hadn't left. All she knew of him was that he'd played rugby at university before the war and now was Australia-bound.

"No. Screwbacks don't just fall off."

"I cannot wear only one earring." Savina began removing the eardrop.

"Pearls aren't that expensive," Phoebe Drake said.

Surprised at the woman's appearance, Isabella looked around. Only then did she realize that the saloon had emptied. A couple of young men still stood at the bar, but besides their cluster, the people had left. "Savina, is that an Imperial topaz?"

"Of course, it's an Imperial. I don't wear cheap stones."

"It looks to be a whole caret," Ingram judged. As the son of a wealthy financier, he could afford to know the size and value of jewels.

"It is," the young woman snapped.

Lionel Wexford's conversation about Lady Bernhardt's necklace also applied to this eardrop. "Then the earring is valuable and easily broken apart for sale. The pearl, the reddish topaz, and the gold setting."

"The thief," Werthy said heavily.

"Exactly," Mrs. Drake said, and Isabella recognized their brief short-hand as a clue that Emerson Werthy and Phoebe Drake knew each other better than she'd realized.

"A thief?" Savina clapped a hand over her mouth. "Like the one that stole Lady Bernhardt's necklace?"

"And my tie pin," Clive Rexford added quietly.

She knew that tie pin, a bezel-cut ruby of thumbnail size, surrounded with pavé diamonds. It had glittered at her over the bridge table on many a night. "I didn't know we'd had thefts until Mr. Wexford told me as we danced."

"Your head is usually in your sketchbook," Phoebe Drake said. "No offense intended."

"None taken. It's true. When did these thefts start?"

Werthy turned and took away her wine glass, setting it on a side table. "When we boarded in Jeddah."

"The thief boarded then? We've only been aboard five days."

"A fast worker. That glorious diamond necklace would be treasure enough."

"But he's also taken my tie pin." Clive Rexford scowled. "The piece is a family heirloom, for which I treasure it, but it's quite valuable on its own."

"And now my earring!"

"There may be other thefts we don't know about," Werthy finished. "You had the earring when we danced, Savina. Who were your partners after?"

"Here now," Mr. Kennedy protested. "That earring may have fallen off. You didn't even search for it."

"Search then. Did Savina have it on when you danced with her, Kennedy?"

"I was looking into her eyes, not her ears."

"Silly." Savina giggled. "You weren't looking into my eyes. But I did have it after our dance because I looked in that mirror." She pointed to the mirror, an expanded oval surrounded by carved and gilded wood. "That was the third dance, before Mrs. Tarrant came in."

"And there were five dances after that."

"Six," Werthy corrected her, and Isabella's face flamed. "Who were your partners after the third dance?"

"We should look for the earring before we accuse anyone." Robin Kennedy's heavy brows drew down. The boyish mop of auburn curls contrasted with his pugnacious air.

"Then we'll look." Phoebe patted his arm, matronly rather than her usual insouciance. "We'll all look."

With the help of the whisky-drinking men and the two stewards, they scoured the saloon. The earring remained lost. The unknown men collapsed into chairs rather than stand and sway. The stewards remained, noncommittal as they closed the bar. When even Kennedy admitted it wouldn't be found, he suggested that someone saw it, pocketed it, and would turn it into the ship's purser in the morning.

"Why not turn it over to Ashish here? Or Patel?" Kennedy had no rebuttal, so Werthy turned to Savina. "Have you remembered your partners?"

Tears threatened to spill from the beauty's over-bright eyes. "Mama will be so angry."

Isabella bumped her arm. "I'm certain you can remember. Did you dance with Col. Werthy first or second?"

She blinked away her tears. "First. Emerson always dances with me first."

"Who was next?"

She scrunched her nose. "Mr. Michaels."

"He's a surprisingly good dancer, isn't he? And you danced third with Mr. Kennedy."

Savina giggled. "That's right."

Gradually, she recalled her other five partners: Mr. Wexford, Mr. Ingram, Mr. Rathburn, Mr. Lear, and Mr. Gregory.

"And did you go onto the deck with any of them?" Phoebe prompted.

"No. I would not. I'm not fast."

The ship's bells counted off four, and Isabella caught back a yawn at the late hour.

"Come, let's retire for the evening," Phoebe coaxed, draping an arm about the young woman's waist. "Everything will look brighter in the morning. I'm certain your parents are wondering where you are."

At the mention of her parents, the young woman began crying, fat tears rolling down her cheeks. Phoebe enlisted Clive Rexford to escort them to the Fremonts' stateroom.

3

One steward had fastened the windows and stood aside, waiting for them to leave. The other had left. Sheridan Ingram left after a muttered conversation with Col. Werthy.

Isabella stopped another yawn. "Phoebe's right. Everything will look brighter in the morning. We have a starting place for our searches."

"I'm not waiting until morning," Werthy ground out.

"Here now. Who appointed you as policeman?" Robin Kennedy planted his fists on his hips. Still swaying, the two whisky drinkers backed him. They had Kennedy's rugby-suited build, but neither would offer a stout support.

Werthy didn't flinch. He turned smartly and headed out the door.

Isabella caught up to him on the deck. "You're not going alone."

"You're not going at all, Isabella."

"Certainly not, but the captain must be with you. Whoever the thief is will go into the ship's brig, to be turned over to the authorities in Muscat."

He scowled but nodded, and she gave a quick 'thanks be to God' that someone would back him.

Kennedy and the whisky men followed, a troop walking forward to the bridge and the captain's quarters behind it.

A steward's white coat loomed ahead. Hearing their footsteps on the wooden deck, the figure turned, and the lamplight revealed a dark-coated man standing beyond him. Brass buttons reflected the amber light.

Capt. Locke removed a hand from the deep pocket of his coat. "Patel here tells me you suspect we have a thief aboard. Another expensive jewel has been stolen?"

Patel faded back but remained close.

"A topaz and pearl earring," Werthy explained, "along with the other items that were reported stolen."

"Other items? I know Mr. Rexford complained of the loss of his tie pin—."

"Taken from my cabin." The man came out of the shadowed passage to the staterooms.

The captain faced him. "You claimed a steward had taken your ruby."

"Someone gained access to my cabin. Only the steward and I had a key. But if a professional thief is aboard, access to a key means nothing."

"You no longer accuse my stewards, Mr. Rexford?"

"I will keep an open mind, Captain."

Locke turned again to Werthy. "What other items have been stolen?"

"Lady Bernhardt reported her necklace stolen."

"Missing, she said. Stolen, I can believe. What else and when?"

"Just now, a topaz and pearl earring taken from Miss Savina Fremont."

"Expensive cargo. A more secure location would have been the purser's safe."

"That would have been wise before. Now it's too late. Now we must find this thief."

"I agree, Werthy. Where do you propose we look? Patel explained that you searched the saloon. The earring was lost there? Have you narrowed the list of suspects?"

"We have. I can personally vouch for one of the five men. I have strong doubts that another would steal. I propose we search the cabins of the other three, starting with Edgar Lear."

Isabella expected a protest from Kennedy. Although he shifted jerkily, he said nothing. She looked around for the two other men. They had vanished. In a whisky fog, they would not be much help to search or question.

"Mr. Rexford, if you would escort Mrs. Tarrant to her cabin—."

"Kennedy, you do it."

Isabella gaped at Clive Rexford, surprised at his refusal. He hadn't checked if Kennedy would escort her. That young man, alone of all of them, hadn't wanted to accuse anyone falsely. She narrowed her eyes. *Why does Rexford want Kennedy out of the way?*

Did he suspect Kennedy of working with the thief?

Is Rexford working with the thief?

Or is Kennedy the thief? He had opposed any accusation of theft without proof. While Isabella agreed that blind accusations solved nothing, she suspected Kennedy's continued disagreement.

Like the fragments in a kaleidoscope, the shards shifted and reformed, new images, new possibilities.

Caught in those new images. Isabella watched the men walk back along the deck to reach the short passage to the portside cabins.

Kennedy stood with her, breathing heavily. He muttered something then said, "Come on, Mrs. Tarrant. I'll see you to your cabin. You better get some sleep. The night's half-gone." He offered his arm.

She ignored it. "What do you know of Edgar Lear?"

"Not much. Met him when we boarded in Jeddah. Young and ambitious."

"Like every young man aboard this ship."

"That's right. We have to make our way in this world, after it chewed us up and spit us out. With nothing as recompense, mind you, not even the promise of honest work."

Isabella ignored his reference to the late war and the government's neglect of its demobbed soldiers. "Have you talked with Mr. Lear?"

"I don't know what you're driving toward, Mrs. Tarrant. Lear and I are not pals, not like you and Werthy and the others. I do know he came off the *Nomadic* with you all. Were there no thefts on that ship?"

She started to explain that accessing cabins on the grand passenger ship was far different than the little thumb-press locks on the *Garipoola*.

A gunshot interrupted her.

Then a shout, several shouts.

Running steps came toward them.

Robin Kennedy thrust her behind him.

A long white jacket ran along the pass-through between the decks. A steward.

Kennedy blocked him.

"Sir! Sir, let me pass!" Patel was wild-eyed and out of breath. "The doctor, he is needed. Urgently." He bolted past as soon as Kennedy moved.

And Kennedy headed into the pass-through. Isabella followed.

Lanterns gave dim illumination to the portside deck. Cabin doors stood open, filled with men in dressing gowns, wives peering over their shoulders. Farther down, Locke stood athwart the deck. He loomed over the slighter Clive Rexford, holding down his arm.

She didn't see Werthy.

A high-pitched yell tore the night. From the bow.

Isabella whirled around.

Two men grappled against the deck rail. Both were dark haired. One still wore his evening suit. The other was shirtless, sweat gleaming on his skin.

Kennedy shoved past her.

Edgar Lear twisted away from Werthy. He sprang for a guy rope to the mast and scrambled up. Werthy grabbed his ankle. He kicked, and the colonel dodged.

Lear scurried up the rope, out of reach. He swung on the line, reached higher, then sprang for the upper deck. The lunge was perfect . . . but the skylight shattered when he landed.

Werthy hesitated then leaped for the ladder fifteen feet beyond to access the upper deck. Kennedy pounded after him. Then Capt. Locke passed her. He swarmed up the steep ladder with the speed of a younger man.

4

Waves crashed against the *Garipoola*. The motor ground on, plowing them toward Muscat. The warm humidity had left the air. Cold wind shivered over Isabella.

Snatches of words reached her. "Go back to bed." "What happened?" "Did we have a stowaway?" "Was that Col. Werthy?" "Why were they fighting?" "Who was shot?"

When she heard that one, she remembered Clive Rexford. He had gone with Werthy and the captain to confront Lear. He was missing now. Where was he?

A cabin door stood open and empty.

She worked through the people still standing on the deck. "I don't know" was all she could answer to their questions. Then she reached the open cabin and peered in.

Rexford searched a suitcase. He'd snapped on all six bulbs, and the garish light hurt her night-adjusted eyes.

"What are you doing?"

He didn't stop. "It *has* to be here. It *has* to be. It's a three-caret ruby. Help me look."

"For your tie pin?"

"For all the missing jewelry." He shoved the suitcase away and turned to the cabinet wall. "They have to be here. He didn't have them on him."

Isabella ventured a step into the cabin. The layout was like hers: bed on one wall, a tiny aisle, the cabinet wall ending in a door that opened to a miniscule lavatory with its sink and WC. Only Lear's cabin reversed the plan, with the lavatory first. She glanced inside but saw nowhere to hide a pouch for jewels.

The pouch wouldn't be large. She eyed the water tank of the WC and peered at the exposed pipes under the sink then closed the door.

"I suppose you fired the shot," she asked as blandly as she could.

"I would have hit him, too, if the captain hadn't knocked my arm down."

"Had you killed him, you would still have no idea where he hid the jewelry. We don't actually know that he's the thief."

He laughed down her reasonable point. "He did it. He's guilty. He wouldn't have tried to run if he were not guilty."

She opened the closet cabinet to reveal suit jackets and trousers. Her skin crawled at searching Lear's clothing, but she dammed her qualms and brought out a dinner jacket to search pockets and lining.

The pockets were empty, but an inner pocket had a faint bit of heft. She pulled out a crumpled handkerchief. When she squeezed the suit fabric, she felt something hard and long. She shoved her hand back into the pocket, testing the seams, and found an inch-long hole. Long enough to slip a small item through the pocket into the lining.

Only it wasn't lining. It was a pocket beside the pocket. Savina's earring slipped out of it as easily as it must have slipped inside.

She drew it out and opened her hand. The Imperial topaz glistened in the garish lighting. The pearl gleamed like the moon.

"Proof," Rexford crowed and resumed searching with greater energy.

Isabella closed her fingers around the earring. She dropped the suit jacket on the bunk and walked out.

The cold night air blew away the ship's coal smoke. Those roused by the gunshot had retired to their cabins.

She kept her fist tightly closed and lifted her hot cheeks to the wind.

Today's storm clouds were long gone, and mere tatters remained, sailing across the gibbous moon.

I should go to my cabin, yet something kept her on that deck, leaning against the wall beside Lear's door, listening to Rexford's growing frustration.

After tonight's interrupted dance with him, Isabella hadn't liked Edgar Lear. Rude was her first complaint. She didn't really know him. He'd sailed with them all the way from Southampton. She didn't even know his friends. She had a vague recollection of his talking with someone on the *Nomadic's* wide boardwalk.

Where did he hide Lady Bernhardt's necklace and the tie pin? Did he take anything else?

Then memory of this afternoon flashed: the crowded lounge, people tucked on the settees or sitting on the floor. And Edgar Lear among them.

He couldn't have stolen the necklace. Multiple people witnessed him in the lounge.

The earring, yes, he did take that. The evidence was in her tightly-closed fist. By the merest chance, its disappearance was spotted before Savina retired for the evening. Because of that, the suspect list had remained small.

Someone else had taken Lady Bernhardt's necklace.

Two thieves, working together. One constructed an alibi while the other stole, then they turned about. They created enough confusion to keep everyone guessing until they could slip away. They had delayed any thefts until after Jeddah, and they worked swiftly and smoothly so that only a few days were needed. What had Capt. Locke called it? *Expensive cargo.* A little web of deceit that reaped great treasure.

They would have traveled on the *Nomadic*, spotting their victims but not acting until the circumstances and the times were ripe. The storm had offered a prime opportunity. Passengers and stewards trapped in place by the storm, and the thief could take his time.

Who else would the thieves have targeted? The storm had lasted hours. How many people had the thief robbed? Isabella wore her jewelry—the gold cross and chain from her father and Madoc's gold wedding ring. Several passengers had fine pieces, not high in value yet still worth pretty little sums. Lady Saunders, though, had a sapphire and diamond brooch. *Does she have it still? Or has it gone missing, and she hasn't yet realized?*

That shadow in the lounge window—.

She closed her eyes, but the memory refused to clear.

"Isabella?"

Her eyes flashed open. Werthy had returned. The lantern cast strange shadows on his face, deep lines and hollows. Richard Owen stood at his shoulder, less haggard and grieved. "Edgar Lear?" she asked, fearing the worst.

"Dead. He fell through the glass skylight of the lounge."

"I found Savina's earring in his suit jacket." She opened her fist to reveal it. The topaz sparkled. The pearl gleamed.

"Give it to her in the morning." He glanced at the open cabin door.

"Mr. Rexford is still searching for his tie pin. Did Mr. Lear say . . . anything . . . before—?"

"He laughed at fate. Said we would find nothing. That was it." He turned to look over the ocean. Reaching into his jacket, he withdrew his cigarillo case. Then he stopped, staring at the silver case as if he'd forgotten its purpose.

"No," she agreed, "we won't find anything except this earring . . . unless we find his accomplice."

That broke his distraction. "What?"

"Edgar Lear didn't work alone. When Lady Bernhardt's necklace was stolen, he was in the lounge, with quite a lot of us to give him an alibi."

"A partner." He extracted a cigarillo then reached for his matches. "Someone we would never expect." The match flared, the tip of the thin brown cigar began to glow, then he tossed the match into the ocean.

The little flame winked out before it reached the water.

"We'll have to work fast." Owen stared along the line of closed cabin doors. "We've only twenty-four hours to find them. More like twenty hours. We'll need a trap."

"I saw someone," Isabella said hurriedly, "on the deck during the worst of the storm."

"Who? Can you draw them?"

"I didn't see him clearly, but—maybe?"

"We could lure them in," Owen proposed. "Lady Saunders has a high-value piece of jewelry. A thief would be a fool not to try for it. That diamond and sapphire brooch."

Werthy's eyes half-lidded. She barely saw their ice-grey glint. "That's one type of trap."

Isabella didn't share her plan for a sketch of the shadowy man. A dreamtime sketch. It might not work. It had before, when she recalled the scene of Tommy Gresham's murder on the Malvaise estate. She had needed more than one sketch to find the right details for Inspector Wainwright.

Capture that sketchy image, and they had a direction for their search—or for their trap.

5

First, Isabella snatched some sleep, mainly because her hands shook with stress and exhaustion.

With morning light flooding through the little round window of her cabin, she began drawing.

The steward brought coffee, but Isabella wasn't interested in breakfast. Her task consumed her. The first sketch was rough, a mere impression, the first shadow that she'd seen, a dark profile.

The image she wanted, the one she needed, was the shadowy face plastered against the lounge windows. When she tried to envision the face, nothing would come. She concentrated on the rain sluicing down the glass.

Her second effort resulted in a bleary blob that could have been anyone.

She focused on the watery streaks, the salt water splashed onto the glass. The wooden frames of the windows were the only definite strokes of her pencil. The face continued to elude her.

She drank water, sharpened her pencils, then paced a few steps in the narrow aisle between her bed and the cabinet wall. She opened the cabin door and stood on the threshold. The ship rocked. The endless surge of waves hypnotized her.

With the door still open and perched on her bed, she sketched a fourth time. She concentrated on the techniques to convey water, the rippling sluice, the spattering splash. The sheen of the glass panes was difficult to create with pencil. A slight unfocus of her inner eye helped capture the drenching rain, the hard window frames, and the negative darkness that separated shadow from light.

The thief was in that negative darkness.

Isabella slipped her pencil into the case and splayed her fingers to stretch her hand. The long striking of the ship's bell echoed in memory. She glanced at her little wind-up Baby Ben clock that had served her for a decade. Half-past twelve. Everyone would be at lunch in the dining room or the canteen below decks with only a skeleton crew at stations.

The cry of gulls drew her attention to the restless sea. She focused on the hazy distance. Then, still half-afraid to judge her attempt, she looked at the sketch.

A man stared at her. The man plastered against the window, his face turned away from the wave that had thrust him into the glass. A man she knew.

And now came a crystal memory, two men talking on the wide boardwalk of the *Nomadic*. She'd seen them in the early days of the voyage, before she knew either of them. They had stood at the deck rail while the ship left La Rochelle. Behind them was an ancient fortress of the old harbor.

She knew both men now. Edgar Lear and Lionel Wexford.

She headed for the bridge. Werthy would be there, trying to convince the captain to trap the thief.

The decks were curiously empty with everyone else at lunch. She spotted a sailor scrambling around on the deck above the lounge. Repairs had started on the skylight, but she didn't hear any hammering.

As she passed the dark short hallway to portside, she spotted a shadowy figure standing inside. Smoking. Relief flooded her. She wouldn't have to go to the bridge.

Then the cigarette arced away. She caught a flash of white. That wasn't a cigarillo.

And the shadow's shoulders were narrow, even filled out with shoulder pads.

Isabella slowed. He turned, all shadow and darkness. She stopped, preferring to confront the thief than have him at her back.

"Good morning, Mrs. Tarrant."

"Good morning, Mr. Wexford."

"We missed you at breakfast. Were you sketching? I suppose you've finished."

"I have, yes. You know what happened to Mr. Lear," she countered.

"Tragic, really. So young and hale, and now so dead."

She flinched at the callous tone. *How do I respond to that?* She didn't try. "I'm late for luncheon."

"Wait."

"Wait? But I missed breakfast."

"Yes, wait. At breakfast this morning, Col. Werthy was very explicit about your sketch." He stepped into the sunlight. His narrowed eyes and flared nostrils were at odds with his dapper straw boater and summer jacket. The wind tugged at his old school tie. "You are the only eyewitness to the second thief." He gestured to her sketchbook, the pages fluttering with the wind racing through the passage. "And that's your only evidence."

She made the mistake of glancing down.

He sprang, and she had no time to protect herself. He ripped away the sketchbook. Then he propelled her backward, against the wooden deck rail. He bent her spine over the rail. Saltwater splashed on her face as the ship rushed through the sea. Then he was wrenched away and pummeled. Isabella sank to her knees as sailors swarmed them.

Wexford shouted and strained against multiple hands, but the sailors had him fast. They towed him forward, past her, to the open bulkhead of the ship's bowels.

Richard Owen crouched beside her. "Are you hurt, Mrs. Tarrant? My apologies. I had orders not to let him touch you, but I didn't expect him to attack from the passage."

He helped her stand then steadied her against a cabin wall before going to fetch her sketchbook. When he came back into the sunlight, he glanced down. The sketchbook remained open to her fourth drawing.

He handed it over with a wry look. "We don't really need an eyewitness sketch now. Wexford showed his hand. Werthy's plan worked."

"His plan was to use me as bait? That man!" Isabella was proud that her voice didn't tremble. "Where is everyone?"

"Saloon or dining hall. Or their cabins. All under orders to keep off the decks until the skylight is repaired."

Setting me up as an easy victim. Tears pricked. "Where is Nedda?"

"Ingram's secretary?" He peered at her. "You're not going to cry, are you?"

She wanted to. She was shaken and jittery, and pain points had started on her arms and waist. "No," she denied. "I want lunch and coffee. In my cabin. Would you ask a steward?"

"Sure. You—uh—want to talk to anyone else?"

"Only Nedda. And only if she's not working. And I want to thank you, Mr. Owen. I do believe you saved my life."

"Worse comes to worse, he would only have tossed you in the water. Captain said it would be nothing to pick you up. I didn't mean to let him put his hands on you, Mrs. Tarrant."

Only tossed me in the water! "Best-laid plans and all that, Mr. Owen. I'm just grateful that the plan didn't go completely awry."

The coffee, strong and black, helped. Soup and poached fish with lemon and buttery rice helped even more.

She cut the eyewitness drawing from her sketchbook and set it aside for the authorities, evidence against Mr. Wexford. The steward agreed to take it to Capt. Locke.

Nedda appeared in the late afternoon. "Come with me," she demanded. "We'll reach port in an hour or two, and I have to pack now. Mr. Ingram plans to leave ship for a hotel as soon as possible."

Isabella had had enough of plans, but she followed her friend to her cabin and helped fold clothes and stow items away.

Nedda recounted Werthy's pronouncement at breakfast. "Very commanding, he was, too, backed up by Capt. Locke."

"I'm surprised no one protested."

"A few did. I'm certain Lionel Wexford wanted to. Edgar Lear's death, though, stopped the protesters. No one wanted to be caught ogling the place of his death."

"Did they recover the missing jewelry? Lady Bernhardt's necklace and Mr. Rexford's tie pin?"

"Found in Mr. Wexford's cabin, in a pouch in the water tank above the WC. Quite drowned. I would never have thought to look there. Apparently, the captain convinced Mr. Wexford to tell his hiding place. He returned their jewelry."

Somehow, Isabella doubted the captain had convinced Lionel Wexford of anything. "I'm certain they were very glad to have their jewelry restored."

"Mr. Rexford was speechless, which was a treat to see. I don't think he's ever been caught with nothing to say. Isabella, you'll have to give a statement to the authorities about Wexford's attack."

"I doubt it. Oman is a Muslim nation and very conservative. Women do not speak to anyone outside the family."

Nedda propped a hand on her hip. "How do you know that?"

"You forget my father's specialty."

She dropped the pose. "Well, Mr. Ingram will demand his secretary's presence at every meeting. His demands are always met. I will speak only to him."

An hour later, with twilight deepening after a spectacular sunset, the *Garipoola* docked, and the local police marched up the narrow gangplank that only sailors used. Having been notified by radio, they went straight to the bridge. As expected, she wasn't called to give any testimony. She wondered if Capt. Locke had handed over the sketch that she had sent him. A quarter-hour later, the police marched away, a disheveled Lionel Wexford amongst them.

Still on deck, Isabella waved a white scarf for her last goodbye to Nedda and the Ingram entourage. They climbed into motorcars idling on the dock, its few lanterns barely competing against the night's blackness. She caught the scent of rich tobacco, so she continued waving long after the motorcars rumbled off the wooden dock.

When she turned, Werthy stood a foot away, smoking one of his ever-present cigarillos. "You'll have to give that up if ever you go into covert work," she warned.

His eyebrows rose. He examined the thin cigar then placed it between his lips, inhaling deeply. "A reason to avoid any covert operation."

The ship's bell rang twice. Seven o'clock and time for dinner. She turned toward the dining room and didn't protest when he fell into step beside her.

"I'm forgiven then?"

She didn't answer.

He sent the half-smoked cigarillo over the rail then held open the dining room door. "What must I do?"

"Not use me as bait in any of your traps. No matter how expedient it is."

"Have I blotted my copybook with you, Isabella? Or should I say Mrs. Tarrant?"

"Mrs. Tarrant will do. Oh, look. Savina is waving. I believe she wants you to join her table. Good evening, Col. Werthy."

He gave one level look then walked away.

Isabella ignored the pang in her heart.

The evening had two saving graces. Wearing the intricate diamond necklace, Lady Bernhardt insisted that Isabella dine with her and the Saunders until they reached Bombay.

Once more Clive Rexford's tie pin sparkled at her over the bridge table. She partnered the mutton-chopped Mr. Fullerton, and they took all the tricks in a game.

Red Mask

1

Isabella stopped at a cloth covered with carved bowls. The vendor had placed the bowls rim-down, to display the carvings of monkeys, elephants, and swirls. Intrigued, she knelt for a closer look.

The bowls spanned a wide spectrum of wood tones, light to dark. She touched a light-colored bowl with monkeys in palm trees. "What is this wood?"

"Sagwan." He repeated it. When she touched a rose-colored wood with little carving but lovely arches, he said, "Sheesham, sheesham." He hovered his hand over a series of bowls. "Nilambur" was a mandala. "Nagpur" had columns like a palace collonade. Tigers slinking through reeds was "Mango."

"And cedar" she named the rust-red bowl.

He plucked the bowl off the ground cloth and turned it upright. Warmed by the sun, the redolent cedar reminded her of clothes presses and chests. Elephants with lifted trunks paraded around the bowl balanced on his hand.

"May I?" She extended her hand.

He bobbed his head. Dark hair fell over his forehead. "You look. You look good." Like any merchant from ages old, he knew touching the product would often sell it.

Closer inspection revealed that each elephant wore a headband and a cloth over its back, this one ornamented with beads, that one with cross-hatches, a third with swirls, and all parading before a different background. The elephant with flowers marched before a temple; the one with cross-hatches walked through a jungle. Eight elephants in all, which the missionary Miss Harlow had claimed was a fortunate number.

Isabella hadn't found anything that called to her like these elephants. Within a few minutes, she owned the bowl, and the vendor grinned from ear to ear. She had likely paid too much, but she had no taste for haggling over a price. Mindful of Col. Werthy's advice at the market in Bombay, before they'd parted ways, she had halved the man's amount. He countered, she paid, and they were both happy with the transaction. The vendor even wrapped the bowl in a vivid green cloth.

When she stood, a passerby knocked into her. She stumbled.

A hand from nowhere steadied her. "Missy good?" her vendor asked.

"Yes, I'm fine. Thank you," she directed at the man, but he was gone.

The vendor settled cross-legged at the back of his cloth. Isabella stepped into the flow of the market and let the current take her forward.

The artist in her loved the vivid colors of the canopies over the booths and open shop fronts. Saffron yellow, emerald green and spring green, poppy red and persimmon, tangerine and heavenly azure, and peacock blue, the colors rioted along both sides of the street. The myriad objects for sale, the varied faces of the vendors, male and female, all started a longing to capture the market with its energy. She would need oils. Watercolors would be too diluted. She yearned for a faster paint than oils or the ability to take color photographs. In black-and-white snapshots, the market would look a crowded mess.

A man in pristine white loose jacket and trousers bumped into her. When she edged over, he remained plastered to her shoulder. "Are you on the *Garipoola*?"

His British accent surprised her as much as his knowledge of her ship. Isabella gaped at him.

"Are you?"

"Yes."

"You know Col. Werthy?"

He had sherry brown eyes, a long narrow face, heavy eyebrows, and swept-back black hair. A beard had started on his defined jawline.

"You know the colonel?" he persisted.

"Yes."

"Good." He thrust a folded paper at her.

"He left the ship in Bombay, with his friend Richard Owen."

"This is for you. Take it," he ordered when she remained reluctant. "You must return to the ship. Hire a rickshaw. Here, I call one for you."

Isabella clutched the folded note. *Do I trust this man?*

When he turned away, she faded into the crowd. As a western woman, blonde and pale, she would be quickly spotted in this crowd of natives. She cast to the other side of the street and hastened back the way she'd come. The current took her until she spotted a landmark that would lead out of the market.

Outside of the bustling market, she would be even more noticeable, and she hurried along the shop fronts. When she happened upon a rickshaw discharging a passenger, she crossed to the rickshawallah. "Harbor? The ship *Garipoola?*"

"Yes, Missy."

"How much?"

He looked offended. "Pay at end."

The rain started as she settled onto the wooden seat. She leaned back to stay under the umbrella canopy. The man picked up the iron bars and began pulling.

As the rain fell, cooling the heated air, his speed increased. Bare feet splashed through the forming puddles, undeterred while others sought shelter from the sudden monsoon rain. Streams poured along the streets and became freshet floods as the deluge continued. Thunder rumbled, but the rickshawallah never paused.

Her skirt was soaked when they reached the harbor. The man ran all the way to the *Garipoola*'s mooring. He offered to carry her up the gangway but didn't seem offended by her refusal. By the time Isabella paid him and reached the ship, she was soaked through. Then, in a twist almost anticipated, as she climbed the gangway the rain stopped, God closing the tap.

From the ship, she looked back at the wharf. Her rickshawhallah was running back to the city, his rickshaw bouncing behind him. A woman had emerged from the port office. A western woman. Then raindrops peppered down, and Isabella hurried to her cabin.

She didn't slip the note from her purse until she changed from her wet clothes, hanging them in her lavatory to drip dry. Then she unwrapped her bowl and added the green cloth to the shower rod. The elephant bowl fit perfectly on the tiny table jutting from the wall by the head of her bed. She tucked her little alarm clock under the shade of the bed lamp. Only then did she unfold the note.

It didn't make sense.

A bottle of whisky should cover the cost. Bring it with you. The red man won't expect the change. Better to have the switch ready. Whiskers shouldn't delay. A cold clime awaits him if we don't succeed. Dead men have skeletons.

At the last sentence, a cold chill ran over her.

A flourishing *W* was the signature.

Is a page missing? But no, the writing didn't cover the sheet.

The man had used Werthy's name. *Is* **W** *my Col. Werthy?*

Werthy *was* a spy—along with Richard Owen and Sheridan Ingram. Yet they had disembarked, Ingram in Muscat, Werthy and Owen in Bombay.

Other spies could still be aboard the *Garipoola*, traveling together to their assignments in the Orient.

Dead men have skeletons.

With that line, the note acquired sinister and lethal meaning. Had the note been meant for a spy? *Did that man mistake me for a spy?* Isabella wanted to laugh, but danger prickled over her. He had mistaken her for someone. A woman on the *Garipoola*. A blonde?

Savina Fremont was blonde, but that young lady could not be the spy. The divorcée Edwina Bridgewater was a platinum blonde from the bottle, with dark lashes and penciled eyebrows to highlight her eyes. Good sense ruled against the flirtatious Mrs. Bridgewater as a cool-headed spy.

Or would that be the perfect cover for a spy? A little frittery, a lot man-crazy, her conversation revolving around fashion and society gossip. Isabella would never have given any suspicion of spying a second thought.

The other blondes aboard were married. Lady Saunders. Mrs. Malcolm, a greying blonde. Mrs. Reynolds, bound to Australia with her family. At least three other women along with the women in third-class. Were the husbands a decoy? She found herself second-guessing everything she knew about several passengers.

This note was obviously in code. Did it talk about four people or three? The red man. Whiskers. The *him* avoiding a cold climate—Siberia? She'd heard the Bolsheviks sentenced prisoners to the frigid north. The fourth would be the skeleton. The *him* and the potential skeleton might be the same person.

The recipient made the fifth person—or fourth. Obviously, the red man was a contact—with a lead to the *him*. And did Whiskers assist the recipient, or was he a threat to keep the note's recipient from delaying?

Ship's bell rang off the time. She counted the strikes even as she checked the time on her little alarm clock. Dinner would be in a half-hour. Her stomach growled in response.

She could puzzle out this note for her evening's entertainment. Mr. Fullerton had already told her that he would not be available tonight for their usual game of bridge. Since Clive Rexton had abandoned them in Bombay, a worthy third and fourth for bridge were hard to find.

As Isabella re-folded the note, she remembered the poison pen letter stolen from her cabin—oh, ages ago, it seemed. A single line had warned her not to encourage Col. Werthy. She had ignored that warning, and Werthy had turned into a good friend. (Too good of a friend, her heart reminded, but she ignored that, too.)

Stealing a letter twice on one voyage—that wouldn't happen. Besides, Savina Fremont had penned the earlier letter then stolen it back. The young woman had remained in hot pursuit of Werthy throughout the voyage, but he hadn't looked back when he left the ship. Savina didn't have anything to do with this note.

Perhaps, just perhaps, she might find a clue about the intended recipient, a blonde woman on the *Garipoola*.

The ship would cast off late tonight and start its journey up the Indian coast to Madras where Isabella's husband, Madoc, waited for her. That was a better focus than a cryptic letter she would never decode.

She refolded the note and placed it in the elephant bowl, weighting it with a piece of jade that Werthy had given her when they parted. Then she dressed and dawdled her way to the Dining Room. She was successfully late.

Dinner found her eying the several blonde women aboard from a new perspective. She dismissed the married couples. Lady Bernhardt and the Saunders commanded the best table, but Isabella hadn't joined them since Bombay, preferring the Australia-bound Reynolds, solid working-class and eager for the opportunities in a new land. She'd introduced fellow immigrant Robin Kennedy to them. They talked so much about the next ship they would board in Madras that they didn't notice Isabella's distraction.

When she returned to the cabin, only the jade piece was in the bowl. The note had vanished.

2

Isabella wanted to kick herself. She should have kept the note with her. She should have known—! The thumbpress locks on the cabin doors wouldn't keep out any determined person.

She caught a whiff of sandalwood, but it was faint, dissipating quickly after she shut her door.

Which blonde woman had invaded her cabin? No one had arrived later than she to dinner although several had left before she did. The late-evening dancing had ended after the lounge's skylight had been broken. Although it had been partially repaired in Bombay, the dancing hadn't resumed. Conversation remained sadly flat, even with Savina Fremont, Mrs. Bridgewater, and a few others trying to enliven the evenings. The reading room was too small for a large gathering.

The endless voyage had bored the passengers, with everyone anticipating the *Garipoola's* last stop in Madras. They would all disperse there for the next stage of their journeys. Isabella and a few would remain in Madras. The Fremonts and others were bound for Hong Kong. The Australian immigrants would embark on their journey's last stage. Not a single passenger would remain aboard for the return trip to Jeddah and parts west.

She picked up the jade and rolled it between her fingers. Who could have taken the note?

A better question: who knew she'd gone to the market? The passengers had a choice of two excursions. With a palace and gardens available, a temple, the beach, and the market, few had picked the market. Any other western women had gone on the official tour of the market in the morning hours. A hotel offered a sedate luncheon.

Isabella had visited the temple first. Then she joined the young men crowding onto a transport to the town center. They had wanted to find other amusements. Robin Kennedy hadn't wanted to leave her alone to explore, but he was easily encouraged to his own pursuits. The British Raj had a strong presence in Cape Cormorin, and Capt. Locke had assured all the passengers that the town was safe.

And she had been safe. The man who'd given her the note made no overt threat. Only intuition had sent her scurrying away. But why would he threaten her since she was his expected contact?

Am I seeing shadows where none exist? I am over a month from England, in time and distance and culture. Maybe the differences bothered her more than she realized.

While she hung up her dinner dress and slipped on her nightgown, she gave herself a lecture. She turned off the overhead lights and the lamp on the ledge desk at the foot of the bed. Then she headed into the tiny lavatory to brush her teeth. She clicked on the light. Nothing happened.

She clicked it off and back on several times. "Oh, bother." The steward would have to replace the bulb in the morning. For tonight, she could leave the little door open and use the desk lamp for light.

She stepped out to turn on the lamp.

A rustle, a whoosh, heavy footsteps—then a shove that thrust her into the chair at the desk. The force bent her over the chair back.

"Ow!" She righted herself.

The person fumbled for the door latch.

She angled the lamp, and light streamed to the door.

A man.

Not a blonde woman.

He ripped the door open and plunged into the darkness on deck.

Isabella dashed after him.

He had vanished, into the short passage between starboard and port. The amber lanterns gave enough light to find the way in the dark. The stewards in their white jackets were beacons in the blackness—but no one was on deck. A sailor shouted, toward the ship's bow, yet he wasn't in sight.

She retreated to her cabin and turned on the overhead lights then sank onto the bed, all atremble.

That man had lurked in the lavatory while she changed.

She hadn't recognized him. He was a dark jacket, dark hair. Not once had she seen his face. She had an impression of height and power, but she had no evidence for that. He'd hunched as he clawed at the door latch. She didn't even know his height. No sketch could recover what she hadn't seen.

And she had no real support on ship.

The jewelry theft had proved Capt. Locke wanted a *fait accompli* before he acted. Emerson Werthy and Richard Owen were long departed. The forceful Lady Peverell would be on her return voyage to England. Lady Bernhardt was nothing like the dowager, and the Saunders—.

Her mind stuck on the Saunders. Lord and Lady, idle rich like the Stropefords. Quite independent of each other, unlike the newly-married Stropefords. So independent that they didn't act like a couple. That wasn't uncommon among the rich, yet when Lord Saunders assisted his wife, he was awkward. That awkwardness didn't extend to his treatment of Lady Bernhardt when he accompanied her along the rocking deck or assisted her to her chair or steadied her on the gangway to the dock.

What am I thinking? That Lord Saunders is not married to Lady Saunders? I've this idea on nothing more than observation?

Lady Saunders was a blonde. A honey blonde, quite unlike Isabella's paler blonde or Savina Fremont's golden curls. Still—she was blonde.

Husband and wife did share a stateroom.

Isabella's former cabinmate from the *Nomadic*, Caro Marten, was Lady Saunders' maid. She would know the relationship between them.

But—her thoughts stuck, frozen to ice. When she'd climbed the gangway and looked down at her rickshaw puller, Caro Marten had emerged from the port office.

And Caro had pale blonde hair.

How did I forget that?

Because Caro stayed in third class. She ate in the canteen belowdecks. She emerged to serve Lady Saunders.

Isabella huffed at her wild ideas. "I'm weaving a conspiracy from the flimsiest of threads."

She wanted her friend Nedda Cortland there, to listen to that wildness and talk sense into her racing brain.

She wanted Werthy's ruthless logic. If nothing else, he would pick apart her scrambled ideas until she could see the sense or nonsense.

Hoping for a clearer head by morning, Isabella finished preparing for bed. The lavatory was filled with a faint clean scent, like Earl Grey tea and white flowers, not gardenia but something else. She splashed her face then flicked off the lamp before tucking into bed. First, though, she positioned her chair under the door knob, to stop any intruder.

Her mind raced, refusing to settle.

The man who'd stolen the note remained on ship.

What exactly had the note said?

The red man.

In India, red was associated with marriage. Before she had disembarked in Bombay, the missionary Miss Harlow had regaled anyone who would listen with her spotty information about Indian culture. Isabella had learned that elephants with lifted trunks meant good fortune. Brides wore red saris. On entering their new homes, they stepped in red paste then left their footprints all through the house.

This, though, was a red man, not a bride. Fire-red—had Miss Harlow said that meant a message from the gods?

The Times had had a blazing headline about a deputation of parliament ministers with the Hands-Off Russia committee. They had visited the Japanese ambassador in London. She'd glanced at the story under the headline while Mr. Malcolm scanned the business columns inside the newspaper.

The Bolsheviks were red. The Russian civil war had divided the country into the red army and the white armies, the latter a loose coalition of Tsarists and nationalists.

She didn't want to think about war.

Yet she knew spies were positioning themselves around the Orient, looking and listening for any threat to Britain.

Was the red man a Russian spy? A defector? Someone stopping a defector?

The previous puzzles she'd solved, blackmail and poison pen letters and jewelry theft, those seemed innocent crimes compared to spying.

Who was Whiskers? Isabella could remember only the name.

The plantation manager had a Van Dyke beard. Of the younger men, two had mustaches. Mr. Rathburn had a neat beard. *Who else?*

Her bridge partner Mr. Fullerton had mutton-chop whiskers. If ever he shaved that out-of-date beard, Isabella doubted she would recognize him. She'd twitted Werthy, ages ago, about not looking at the people around him, but she doubted she could identify a clean-shaven Fullerton. How many nights had she sat across the bridge table as his partner? She'd seen only his bushy eyebrows and whiskers. His eye color escaped her. She didn't recall anything about his nose. Straight? Roman? Thin? Pinched? Those mutton chops identified him to everyone.

Shaved, he could disappear, and no one could identify him.

Fullerton might be Whiskers, working against the unidentified red man. A Russian Federalist spy.

And why do I think Whiskers is aboard? Neither the red man nor Whiskers had to be passengers. They could be in Madras, the *Garipoola*'s final stop.

What else had the note said? Something to exchange. A person? A defector? Madoc had described an exchange of prisoners of war, one of his few accounts of his wartime service. She imagined just such a tense situation.

Had the note said *exchange*—or *change*? "The red man won't expect the change," she recalled. That didn't have to be a person. An item. A vital piece of information. Something as mundane as a clock.

And a fifth of whiskey—no, a bottle of whisky. *Why do I have a fifth in my head?* A fifth was an American measurement. This was a bottle of whisky.

She tossed over. The sheets had tangled around her legs. She fought free and dragged the chair away to open the door. The night air welcomed her and cooled her spinning brain.

The *Garipoola* had left the lights of Cape Cormorin far behind and steamed into the coastal sea lanes.

Is **W** *my Col Werthy?*

Springing from the depths of her mind, that thought perturbed her. He wasn't *her* Col. Werthy. He was long gone. Isabella doubted she would ever see him again. She looked forward to her reunion with Madoc and the adventures she'd have in India and Australia.

She flounced back into her room, flicked on the light to reset her chair under the door knob. Then, fingers on the lamp pull, she glanced at her alarm clock to see how much of the night she'd wasted on the mysterious note and people that she would soon leave behind.

Her trusty Baby Ben alarm clock had vanished.

She looked on the floor and felt around the platform that supported the mattress. The cabin had no corner or cranny for the little clock to roll into.

It was gone.

Only the intruder could have taken it.

3

The steward informed Isabella that Mrs. Justin Drake broke the fast in her cabin and didn't emerge until mid-morning.

She parked on a shaded deck chair that gave a view of Mrs. Drake's cabin. She passed the time by sketching the Hindu temple she had toured in Cape Cormorin then noted plans for a last watercolor commemorating her voyage.

By ship's clock it was after ten when Phoebe Drake came along the deck from the cabins. In a fluttering blouse and matching skirt of seagreen silk, she looked coolly sophisticated. A simple teal purse swung from her shoulder.

Isabella hastily stowed her pencils and snapped shut her sketchbook. She twisted her satchel's strap to a short length. As the svelte woman reached her, she stepped into her path. "May I have a word, Mrs. Drake?"

Kohl-lined brown eyes surveyed Isabella, emphasizing the contrast of her pale skin and dark hair. "It's too early for such a serious question."

"We can talk up there." She motioned to the deck beyond the Reading Room, where the walkway narrowed before it reached the Dining Room then the lounge, still off-limits while the sailors finished repairs to the skylight.

"I see no reason—."

"Did you ever work with Col. Werthy?"

Her finely-drawn eyebrows lifted then lowered. By no other expression did she reveal the impression that single question had.

Voices interrupted them. More passengers came late from their cabins, intent on the Reading Room. Isabella spotted Lady Saunders and Mrs. Bridgewater chattering, walking ahead of Lord Saunders and Lady Bernhardt.

Phoebe Drake strolled past Isabella. "Come along, Mrs. Tarrant."

Waves splashed against the gunwale. The bright sun flashed on the water. Sailors called to each other as they worked on the deck above the lounge. She caught a scent of white flowers as she trailed Mrs. Drake, but it was gardenia, not white jasmine.

And that reminded her of the scent that had filled her lavatory after the intruder had hidden there. Earl Grey tea, she'd thought. That was bergamot. The smell was something more, jasmine and—the aroma lurked, but she couldn't name it. Mr. Fullerton, her bridge partner, used heavy sandalwood. Col. Werthy had worn a light fragrance, balsam and cedar with a hint of lavender. Where had she smelled that scent? It was recent, several days running, but she couldn't place it.

The woman stopped beyond the windows of the Reading Room, crowded this morning. She extracted a cobalt blue holder from her purse and a cigarette from an enameled case. "Smoke?"

"No, thank you."

"What do you want then?" She fitted the cigarette into the holder then searched for a matchbook in her purse. Her movements were slow, languid, as if she held countless minutes in reserve. "You mentioned Werthy? Missing him, are you? Do you want his address in Bombay?"

"I had the distinct idea that Bombay was not his destination."

The lit match paused briefly before it touched the cigarette. Phoebe inhaled deeply then shook out the match and dropped it on the deck. "Did he tell you that?"

"He gave no hints of his plans to me. I had only an impression that he would travel inland."

Brown eyes narrowed on Isabella. "You've had several good impressions on our voyage from England."

"One of which was that you worked with him in the past?" She kept the statement as a question.

"Is it vital that you know the answer?"

"Not vital but, in light of a recent circumstance, that knowledge would be—," she chose the word carefully, "reassuring."

"I daresay. I will say only that a certain amount of time has passed since those days."

"Did you know Arabella Swandon before we boarded in Southampton?"

"I do not intend to have a conversation about past acquaintances, Mrs. Tarrant. What recent circumstance has led to this need for reassurance?"

"Yesterday morning, you toured the gardens after you left the market then lunched at the hotel."

She blew a stream of smoke. "And?"

"I received a letter by mistake. A note, really, for it was brief."

"A note?"

"For a woman on the *Garipoola*, a western woman, obviously. I thought I received the note because I am blonde, but it occurs to me that I may have been the only western woman in the market at that time, when the man needed to deliver it. He could have looked for a brunette or a red-head, not just a blonde. Were you expecting a note?"

"Why do you ask me?" she parried.

"The man confirmed that I knew Col. Werthy before he gave me the note."

Phoebe stared at the ocean waters. Ship's bell rang once, sharp and brief, marking the half-hour. Sailors hammered at the broken skylight on the deck above. Somewhere distant, a girlish voice raised in a popular Irving Berlin tune:

All by myself in the morning

All by myself in the night

I sit alone with a table and a chair.

"Was this man English?"

"Indian."

"Not English at all?"

"I don't think I would mistake that."

A smile crept out. Phoebe covered it by returning the blue cigarette holder to her cerise-colored lips. Isabella waited, wanting answers. She leaned on the railing, feeling the occasional splash of saltwater as the ship sped along. The sun blazed down, heating the day which the breeze didn't cool. *Patience*, she reminded and looked into the glittering water.

"What did this note say, Mrs. Tarrant?"

"I can't remember all of it."

"I'll take it, if you would rather not keep it."

She watched the woman closely. Her reaction to this would be telling. "I would love to give the responsibility of it over to you, but I cannot. It was stolen."

Phoebe became absolutely still, not even seeming to breathe. She placed a hand on the pole supporting the upper walkway over the main deck. Like a stiff marionette, she slowly looked around, at the chattering people crowding into the Reading Room. "That is a highly interesting circumstance."

"I thought so."

"What do you remember of it?"

Isabella recited what she could remember: the whisky, the red man, and Whiskers. "Obviously, code."

Phoebe gave an arch look that needed no echo of Isabella's judgement. "We might need that note."

"Would you have an idea who else would need to know about it? For example, you might inform Whiskers that the note is missing and someone unsavory may have it."

"If I knew Whiskers' identity."

It was Isabella's turn for an arch look. "My duty is done." She mimed dusting off her hands.

The girl had lilted up into a song that fit her voice:

> *In my sweet little Alice blue gown*
>
> *When I first wandered down into town*
>
> *I was so proud inside,*
>
> *As I felt every eye,*
>
> *And in every shop window*
>
> *I primped passing by.*

For some odd reason, the song reminded her of the scent. Bergamot and white jasmine and bay, a light *eau de cologne*, clashing with the smell of dinner.

And she knew where she'd smelled it. At dinner, on several occasions after she'd fallen out with Col. Werthy, when she dined with Lady Bernhardt and the Saunders.

4

Twenty-four hours still remained before the *Garipoola* docked in Madras and Isabella re-united with her husband. That excitement didn't distract her from the current puzzle.

She determined that she would have to talk with her former cabinmate Caro Marten, maid to Lady Saunders. That meant she would miss tea.

Isabella had spent a few hours arguing with herself that the intruder to her cabin could not have been Lord Saunders, but that scent of bergamot, jasmine, and bay was too distinct of a cologne not to associate it with him. Most men cloaked themselves in sandalwood or bay or clove. If she hadn't shared a table with the Saunders couple and Lady Bernhardt, she would never have come close enough to smell a cologne so lightly applied.

She didn't know what she expected to learn from Caro. They may have shared a cabin for days, but they hadn't really become friends, not the way she'd become friends with the secretary Nedda Cortland. Part of that was

Caro's position as maid, on call with her employer when Isabella was usually free. She also hadn't become friends with Hettie Rufford, who'd been the fourth in their third-class cabin on the *Nomadic*.

As soon as Lady Saunders joined Lady Bernhardt in the Dining Room, Isabella headed for the staterooms behind the bridge and pilothouse. Lord Saunders would have joined the men in the forward-facing upper-deck Smoking Room. They usually had whisky with cigars while the women indulged in tiny sandwiches and creamy confections.

Caro was the only other blonde not at the hotel for luncheon when the man had searched for his supposed contact. Isabella hadn't seen Caro at the market, but perhaps she'd gone earlier. The woman he looked for would have been a brunette or a red-head, as she'd speculated to Phoebe Drake, but suspicions said no, not when the scent in her lavatory pointed her to the Saunders.

The man had picked Isabella for his contact for a reason. The golden blonde Savina Fremont hadn't visited the market, nor had the other blondes aboard ship, remaining with the tours to the temple, the palace and gardens, and the hotel for lunch. Isabella had skipped the hotel to explore the market. She'd done so alone.

Had that been one of the man's criteria for his contact, a western woman alone?

All the potential threads snarled into a tangle, and she had no guidance to find the right thread to unpick the snarl and work everything loose.

Caro's answer to a couple of questions would help.

A steward pointed her to the Saunders' stateroom. Isabella knocked and waited, hoping Caro had maintained the schedule followed on the *Nomadic*.

The door opened, and Caro peeked around it. Seeing Isabella, the maid opened the door wider. "Mrs. Tarrant. The Saunders are at tea."

"I've come to speak with you, Caro."

"Me?"

"Are you busy?"

The maid glanced over her shoulder then stepped into the passageway, shutting the door behind her. "I have been pressing her ladyship's wardrobe. We leave ship in Madras, you know. We're bound inland."

"We all have to leave ship. The *Garipoola* will steam back to Jeddah. I suppose your tomorrow will be taken up with packing."

Caro scowled, either from the sun in her eyes or at Isabella's interruption. "And unpacking then repacking. Lady Saunders always changes her mind. Did you have something particular to ask me?"

Her questions about the Saunders seemed too intrusive for an abrupt leap to them. "Just—we never talked much, did we, on the *Nomadic*? I've hardly seen you since Port Said."

The maid shrugged. "I work for my living. You do not."

"Have you been in a long employment with the Saunders?"

"What is this? You suddenly want to know about my life when we've less than a day remaining aboard? I doubt we'll ever see each other again."

"The old world's a strange place. We could."

She rolled her eyes. "I doubt it. You're—what? Australia-bound after a few weeks in India? I'll be here for months. In the interior."

"Do the Saunders have a plantation?"

"Tea, I think."

"You don't know?"

Caro folded her arms and leaned against the stateroom door. "I've never been there."

"So, you're not a long-time employee?"

"I have been," she countered. "We were in London and Kent, then Lord Saunders' uncle decided he had to spend time at the family plantation."

Isabella didn't have to fake surprise. "I didn't know that."

"What reason would they have to tell *you*?"

"That seems a strange decree, to require someone who knows nothing about tea or India to uproot family and all to come here."

Caro didn't respond. Isabella flailed around for a next topic. Before she found it, the maid grimaced. "Look, just ask what you want to know. I cannot tell you their financial situation beyond the uncle who holds the purse strings. I don't know their politics. I do know Lady Saunders has her good works society that meets in Charing Cross."

"And Lord Saunders?"

Her shoulders hunched. "He has his club, of course, but I don't have much to do with him."

"He and his wife aren't very ... devoted to each other. He gives more attention to Lady Bernhardt."

"Noticed that, did you? He's more comfortable around the old ladies. That's his way. What else? I need to press Lady Saunders' dress for this evening."

"Where did the Saunders go when we were in Cape Cormorin?"

"The palace and the gardens and the hotel."

"Were you with them?"

"Not me. That was my free time."

"I saw you come out of the port office."

"So, that's it." Caro's blue eyes narrowed. "If you want to know what I did and report it back, you should just ask. I've no secrets."

"I don't report to anyone."

"Don't you? I thought you did, that he left ship in Bombay."

"I don't report to anyone," Isabella insisted.

"Then I'm mistaken," she acquiesced, doubt clear in her voice. "It explained the reason you poked your nose in everywhere."

She opened her mouth to argue then shut it, realizing what Caro believed didn't matter. After tomorrow, they would never again meet. She returned to the important question: *Should Caro have received that note?* "Where did you go when you were off-ship?" Then she recognized that Caro had had nothing to do with Emerson Werthy. *Why would he have sent her a note? He wouldn't have. I shouldn't be here.* What would this mistake cost her?

"The palace and gardens. The market."

"I didn't see you at the market."

She gave a tittering laugh. "Are you checking on *me*? Do you think I'm a *spy*? I'm flattered. Most people ignore those of us in service."

"But—."

"I didn't see you there, either. The rain caught me. I took shelter as soon as I reached the docks. Now, if that's all—." She opened the door behind her and backed into the stateroom. "Ta-ta, Mrs. Tarrant. I hope we *never* meet again."

The encounter unsettled Isabella for the rest of the evening. She barely spoke at dinner, and her mind was certainly not on the bridge game. Mr.

Fullerton called her to book several times.

As she climbed into bed, she placated her perturbation by reminding herself that Phoebe Drake had the important information. Phoebe would know what to do with it and who needed to know.

Isabella suspected this mystery would remain unsolved for her. Phoebe might discover the answer. By tomorrow night, Isabella would be with Madoc and no longer thinking about a note written in code.

5

From sea, Madras looked like other ports of the Far East, teeming with a variety of vessels, the city hunkered behind the wharf, and the heavy clouds of the summer monsoons hanging overhead, a purple shroud in the deepening twilight.

With the other passengers, Isabella watched from the deck rail as the *Garipoola* headed into harbor. Then they all returned to their cabins, to pack the last few things and prepare to leave. Isabella left her cabin door open, ready for the steward to collect her suitcase.

The girl was singing again, back to "Alice Blue Gown", her high thready voice at odds with the shouts of the sailors as they brought the passenger ship to its mooring.

The cabin door swung shut. Before Isabella could turn, a shove propelled her against the cabinet wall. A hand gripped her skull and mashed her face against the polished wood. Bergamot and jasmine filled her nostrils. The long bar of a forearm thrust across her midback. "Where is it?"

"Wh-what?"

"The note. Where is it?"

He clipped his words, precise, sharp. She knew that voice but couldn't place it. The cologne, though, that she knew. Lord Saunders. "I don't have it."

His fingers tangled in her hair. He snapped her head back then banged it forward, into the wood.

"Ow!"

"You'll get worse than that if you don't give it to me."

"I don't have it, my lord Saunders."

He banged her head again. She kicked back, glad she had on sturdy walking shoes, but she missed his leg.

"What the—!"

"I want my clock," she demanded. "Where is it? You took it."

"Overboard." Satisfaction colored his voice. "Now tell me where you hid the note."

Isabella stomped down on his foot, but the angle was wrong and she had no leverage. He punished her by leaning his whole weight against her, forcing air from her lungs. "The note! I'm losing patience."

He lifted back, and she wheezed. "But you took it! When you took my clock!"

"Look here—."

The door slammed open.

Saunders swore. He started to swing her around, between him and the door. Isabella dropped. His fingers yanked in her hair, but she was on her knees and scratching at his hand.

A woman spoke coolly, calmly. "Step away from her. Face the porthole."

From the floor, Isabella gaped at Phoebe Drake. The pistol in her steady hand looked huge.

Squeezing past her was Nelson Fullerton, handcuffs at the ready. Capt. Locke and two sailors loomed outside her door.

Locke and his men took custody of Lord Saunders, and Fullerton reminded them to keep him in the brig until the British authorities took custody of him.

"Our red man," Phoebe said calmly while Isabella rubbed her sore scalp. "We weren't certain of his identity or his ring of assistants."

"Caro Marten, for one."

"You discovered her," the woman agreed. "For which we thank you. We weren't certain. His wife is his other assistant, of course."

"I thought they were upper-crust." Isabella massaged the knot on her forehead.

"They are." Fullerton had returned. "They're also Communists going to set up a station here in India, from which they would add to the unrest in the country."

"You're Whiskers."

"Rather obvious," Phoebe judged. "He'll have to shave."

"Me, shave? No." Yet he grinned, and Isabella guessed those mutton-chop whiskers wouldn't survive the week.

"But why did this happen? Why now? Why the note?"

"We had one last chance to ferret them out before everyone scattered off the *Garipoola*," he explained. "As a plan, it had multiple flaws—."

"And a too-obvious note."

"And Col. Werthy made me bait again," Isabella said bitterly.

Fullerton patted her shoulder. "We knew you. We knew you were trustworthy. You did exactly as Werthy anticipated, when he anticipated."

Phoebe added, "I made the note ominous enough and obscure enough to intrigue you."

Isabella remembered her cold chills at the words *dead men*. "No one is in actual trouble?"

"No, although Werthy and Owen set the word around that a defector wanted contact with one of our agents. They were desperate to discover who the defector was and report that to Moscow. They cabled the Saunders, but I didn't realize the import of that cryptic wire until we were docking in Cape Cormorin. Phoebe and I had to scramble together a plan."

"I did wonder if there was a defector. Who took the note from my cabin? Saunders didn't."

"I did," Fullerton confessed. "I whisked it out of there before he came looking. What put you onto Caro Marten?"

"Nothing did. I was looking for any blonde woman on the *Garipoola* who would have been in the market. Me. Her. Lady Saunders, I thought. Everyone else was at the hotel having lunch or hadn't gone ashore."

"Mrs. Tarrant, I'm going to give you an address." Fullerton's gaze met hers steadily, that head-on look when he tried to convey the importance of his hand at the bridge table. "I want you to memorize it. Anything that strikes you as odd or unusual, you write down, every detail, and mail it to that address. Or send a wire when you deem it urgent. I'll tell them to watch for any communication from you."

"I doubt I will encounter anything, Mr. Fullerton. I mean, my husband is in road building. We'll be in the bush, not a city full of conspirators."

"Just in case," he soothed.

"Send it coded, of course," Phoebe warned. "The wire, I mean."

"Of course."

.~.~.~.

Madoc scooped her into his arms and whirled her around. He kept her tucked close while Isabella said her farewells to the few passengers lingering on the dock.

"Tell me about all the friends you made." He roped her suitcase and trunk to the back of his motorcar. An up-to-date Model T, all the way from America, he'd said when she asked, supplied by Tredennit. "Nothing but the best for his manager. Now, about your friends."

"I'll tell you tomorrow," she promised. "Tonight is for us."

He gave her a glowing smile that warmed everything that had gone cold inside her over the last days. "It is indeed."

Later, much later, when she lay in her sleeping husband's arms, she listened to the monsoon downpour. Phoebe and Fullerton had acted as if the puzzle pieces of their plan had slid easily into place. Isabella knew that hadn't happened. Too easily a flimsy piece could have gotten bent or broken. A piece like her.

Dead men have skeletons. She shivered then resolutely shut her eyes.

Thank You!

Thank you for reading the short stories in the **Sailing with Mystery** series. I hope you've enjoyed this return to the world of Isabella Newcombe Tarrant.

The **Into Death** series featuring Isabella was not the first series that I published. However, the first novel in that series, *Digging into Death*, was my first manuscript under this pen name.

After I published the first Regency mysteries in the **Hearts in Hazard** series, I picked up this novel, doubled the number of suspects, reworked several ideas, and published *Digging into Death* a year after those first three novels. Because of her early advent in my writing plans, Isabella has remained attached to my soul. When I published *Portrait with Death* in July of 2021, I sadly waved goodbye to Isabella and looked forward to writing novels with Flick Sherbourne, the second protagonist in that novel. Those stories are still on the horizon, yet here I am with short stories for Isabella that had not previously entered my plans.

This short story collection is five in number ~ "Amber Dreams", "Purple Poison", "Black Heart", "Silver Web", and "Red Mask". In planning the covers with the project manager for my designer, we had the wonderful idea to use watercolors that represented both Isabella's ocean voyage as well as the atmosphere of the stories.

We hope you enjoy the stories and the covers!

. ~ . ~ . ~ .

For any questions, comments, and speculations, please contact winkbooks@aol.com. Information and links are on the website Writers Ink Books. Look for M.'s titles at online distributors both nationally and internationally.

Please subscribe to M.'s seasonal newsletter for up-to-date information about her fiction and nonfiction as well as recent releases. Contact either winkbooks@aol.com or use the following link to join the newsletter AND receive a free mystery short story >> "The Lion's Den" https://dl.bookfunnel.com/wc84divkre

Please write a review.

Indie writers thrive on freely-given reviews. We're small beans here; we don't have the advertising budget of the Big Peeps. Of course, with *any* book that you enjoy, please share with other readers looking for escape from the dark stresses of life. That's the reason we write.

More Fiction from M.A. Lee

The **Into Death** Series

Featuring the artist Isabella Newcombe

Digging into Death ~ A governess seeking refuge, a handsome young man, an archaeological dig on the island of Crete. Romance is inevitable; murder is not. Suspicions escalate, artifacts are stolen, and then a second murder. Has the love of her life beguiled Isabella straight into death? Available in paperback and e-book

Christmas with Death ~ Christmas is for miracles, merriment, and murder. Set in 1919 at an English country manor for a party throughout Christmastide. Available in paperback and e-book.

Portrait with Death ~ Isabella and her new friend Flick stumble upon the body of George Webberly, a teacher at Greavley Abbey School. Why would anyone kill a school master? Motives abound, and suspects increase. Who committed the murder? Can Isabella find the answer?

These three titles are in the anthology **Into Death**. https://books2read.com/u/baDN1L

Sailing into Mystery ~ Mystery and peril are dangerous shipmates for an ocean voyage.

Isabella travels to rejoin her husband Madoc, currently in India, and encounters puzzles and intrigue.

The collection includes a stolen diary in "Amber Dreams", poison pen letters in "Purple Poison", mischievous pranks in "Black Heart", jewelry theft in "Silver Web", and lethal spies in "The Red Mask".

~ a stand-alone novella with characters from *Christmas with Death*

The Lion's Den ~ Jack Portman had never forgotten Filly Malvaise. Then she walked into his local pub and into the clutches of a loan shark.

Can he rescue her before she falls victim to evil?

The Lion's Den features London in the early 1920s with the Bright Young Things. The returned soldiers of the Great War have settled uncomfortably into their lives.

The **Hearts in Hazard** 12-book series

Regency Mysteries and Suspense with a Dash of Romance

1 ~ *A Game of Secrets* ~ Smugglers, secrets and spies: Kate tries to hide in plain sight; Tony tries to catch a spy. First they fall in love, then they fall into trouble with smugglers. Will they survive? https://books2read.com/u/bPKoZz

2 ~ *A Game of Spies* ~ Salons and soirées, flirtation and dancing, gambling and spies: Josette and Giles fall in love over a deck of cards—and try not to die.

Spymaster Giles Hargreaves was introduced in *A Game of Secrets*.

3 ~ *A Game of Hearts* ~ Two couples :: One titled widow, one wealthy businessman: two hearts shadowed by their past. One bright young flirt, one hard-edged young man: two hearts crossed by circumstance. Mix in a courtesan and two rakes, all out for mischief, and murder bloody and foul.

A Trio of Games ~ a collection of these three novels.

4 ~ *The Danger of Secrets* ~ Deep in the wintry countryside, a house warmed by relatives and friends: secrets of family, secrets of hearts, secrets of blood and pain. Match a daughter to an unknown father; match a spinster to an earl; match a serial killer to his next victim.

Gordon Musgrove was introduced in *A Game of Spies*.

5 ~ *The Danger for Spies* ~ Impossibilities? Rakes don't lose their hearts. Spies don't give up the game. No one hides in plain sight. Codes are unbreakable. A man can't hold onto revenge for years and years. Impossibilities are designed to be shattered.

Toby Kennitt was introduced in *A Game of Spies*.

6 ~ *The Danger to Hearts* ~ A country manor in early Spring: older woman and younger man. Horses, cats, needlework, roses and afternoon teas ~ What could possibly go wrong in an idyll? Trouble in the past, trouble now, and murder.

The character Jess Carter was introduced in *A Game of Secrets*.

A Trio of Dangers ~ the second three Hearts in Hazard titles in a collection.

7 ~ *The Key to Secrets* ~ Debutantes should snare fiancés, not murder

them. Constable Hector Evans must solve three murders. Is his former love guilty, of is she a convenient scapegoat?

Constable Hector Evans was introduced in *The Danger to Hearts*.

8 ~ *The Key for Spies* ~ Spies and traitors. Lies and treachery. Unexpected love where bullets fly. One traitor destroys loyalty. What will two traitors destroy?

9 ~ *The Key with Hearts* ~ A convenient marriage inconveniently causes murder.

A Trio of Keys ~ the third three Hearts in Hazard titles as a collection.

10 ~ *The Hazard of Secrets* .~ Two hearts with dangerous pasts—Can they keep their secrets, or will murder force them to reveal all?

11 ~ *The Hazard for Spies* ~ Disguised to spy. Will murder destroy their chance for love?

12 ~ *The Hazard with Hearts* ~ Two wives haunt the castle. Will she be the third to die?

A Trio of Hazards ~ the fourth three Hearts in Hazard titles collected together.

The **Miss Beale Writes** series

A Touch of Gothic, A Touch of Mystery, A Touch of Romance

The Dark Lord ~ Everyone knows there's no such thing as ghosts. Tell that to the two ghosts haunting Elizabeth.

A mystery novella of Regency England. https://books2read.com/u/38yprZ

The Bride in Ghostly White ~ Unfortunate accident? Or premeditated death? Only the ghost knows, and she's not telling.

A mystery novella of Victorian England. COMING SOON!

Perils in Lace and Hard Iron ~ the two novellas above collected together. COMING SOON!

More novellas in this series ~ coming soon:

The Captive in Green ~ Medieval England

The Prisoner of Stone ~ Tudor England

Perils in Silk and Cold Stone

The Red Monk ~ Restoration England

Moonlight on a Silver Sword ~ Georgian England

Perils in Satin and Sharp Steel

Wild Sherwood

The Historical Legend fused with the Faeries of British Myth

Two Collections from Edie Roones & M. A Lee

Into Wild Sherwood ~ an anthology of five short stories

"Tod the Fox and the Faeries in the Ring" :: *Never enter a Faerie Ring. The Faeries like to play.*

With the guards of Nottingham on his heels, Tod flees to wild Sherwood Forest. Frightened in the night, he falls into a Faerie Ring. Faeries play with their catch, whether in the Ring or on the Wild Hunt. How can he escape them?

"The Poisoner and the Faerie Huntsman" :: *Never reveal weakness to a Faerie.*

Escaping a false accusation of poisoning, Melly and her hound hide from pursuit in Sherwood Forest. That night, she encounters the black hounds of the Wild Hunt. Then the Huntsman arrives. Has she fallen into greater trouble?

"Three Yule Feasts for Faeries" :: *Will the cook become the final dish?*

Yule: the worst time of year for Ellen Best. Then a Faerie knocks at her door. Two dinners, he proposes, and a final feast for his duchess. After each, she'll receive payment. Yet what did the Faerie mean by *final* feast?

"Friar Tuck and the Faerie at the Pool" :: *No one escapes from Faeries.*

Friar Tuck encounters a Faerie at a cool forest pool. She is wondrous and strange and deadly. How can he convince her that he is a man of peace, unlike the guards and rangers who hunt in the forest?

"Alan-a-Dale and the Harp of Elandrielle" :: *Who can trust a Faerie?*

The song competition at Nottingham's Winter Feast offers a purse that will pay Alan-a-Dale's debts. He wins the first night's round … offending his competitors who take revenge. At his lowest point, a Faerie finds him. She offers him a bargain—yet who can trust a Faerie?

Link to this anthology: https://books2read.com/u/bOzoDE

Outlaws of Wild Sherwood ~ another anthology with five short stories

"A Twist of Faerie Magic" :: *A twist of murder. A twist of Faerie magic. And Dav the wrestler caught between.*

When Dav is accused of murdering his true love's husband, will magic reveal the true culprit?

"A Faerie Song for a Feast" :: *Masks, Mummers, and a Faerie Song*

Alan-a-Dale risks playing a song learned in the land of Faeries to help Robin Hood and his men. Will the song help or hinder the outlaws?

"Mischief of a Faerie" :: *A Challenge with Quarterstaves*

When his sister names a bearded giant as her newborn's father, Arthur storms off to force Little John to support them. Yet how can a simple poacher defeat a man taller and stronger than he is?

"The Green Man" :: *A Venture with Destiny*

Bad luck has plagued Jack Greenleaf for years. Abandoned, evicted, and rejected, he joined the other outcasts in Sherwood Forest. The Green Man of the Faerie may seal his fate.

"The Prize of a Golden Arrow" :: *By Hook or Crook or Arrow*

Gil vowed never again to take up the long bow. Then he learns the May Day archery contest is a trap to capture Robin Hood. He resolves to foil the Sheriff's plan.

Link to this anthology: https://books2read.com/u/4Aj99N

. ~ . ~ . ~ .

Edie Roones also writes novellas in the **Wild Sherwood** series. The first one, *The Hooded Outlaw*, features Robin Hood and Lady Marianne. Additional novellas with Will Scarlet, Much the Miller's Son, and Little John will follow.

All books from Writers' Ink are available at online distributors everywhere.

Visit www.writersinkbooks.com

for Quick Links under the author pages for M.A. Lee and Edie Roones.

For any comments, questions, and speculations, contact winkbooks@aol.com. Use the subject line to aim your email to a specific book or series or author.

Words of Praise for Unconditional Remembrance

"*Unconditional Remembrance* is a powerful guide to reconnecting with your inner GPS—your God-Positioning System. Laurie masterfully reveals both the why and the how of deepening your connection to Source, ensuring that everything you create in life comes from the full power of who you truly are."

-Colin Sprake, founder and CEO, Make Your Mark Training and Consulting

"Laurie Seymour shows us how to remember our original connection, to remember our own truth, to remember being aligned with our higher Self. To REMEMBER!"

-Diane Solomon, award-winning author of *Eva* and *The Ravenstone series*

"This is an essential read for leaders who are ready to align with their purpose, embrace their gifts, and co-create from a place of love and purpose."

-Lisa Marie Platske, President, Upside Thinking

"This book is not merely a one-time read; rather, it is felt, lived, and returned to, like a trusted friend on the path of awakening."

-Moshe Gersht, author of the Wall Street Journal and USA Today bestselling book *It's All the Same to Me* and *The Three Conditions*

"*Unconditional Remembrance* is a salve to the soul and brought me to a place of peace and love for myself, and I know it will do the same for everyone who is blessed to read this new book."

-Jennifer Hough, author of Unstuck and founder of *The Wide Awakening*

"*Unconditional Remembrance* will open you to receive a knowing of your unique expression and purpose in this life. Give yourself the gift of knowing who you truly are..."

-Deborah Sandella, originator of the RIM Method and International #1 bestselling author of *Goodbye, Hurt & Pain*

"Laurie Seymour offers not just wisdom, but an energetic transmission that awakens your connection to God within—your Inner Teacher and the guidance provided."

-Anita Adams, author of *Whispers of the Soul* and creator of *The Wisdom Way*

"*Unconditional Remembrance: Your Connection to Source* is a profound book. If you allow it to impact you, you will remember more and more of your original connection with Source."
-Dr. Anita Sanchez (Aztec & Toltec), international award-winning author of *The Four Sacred Gifts: Indigenous Wisdom*

"One of the best 'Must-Read' books I've seen in a while. Throughout *Unconditional Remembrance*, Laurie Seymour invites, teaches, inspires, and provides you with a path to remember the truth of who you are."
-Teresa de Grosbois, #1 international bestselling author of *Mass Influence*

"As Laurie Seymour shares stories from her heart, the truths we all share ring clear as a bell, and we remember what had been forgotten and buried in confusion and doubt."
- Kerri Hummingbird, Medicine Woman, Mentor, and Messenger, #1 international bestselling author of *The Second Wave* and *Inner Medicine*

"This book doesn't offer conclusions. It opens space. You begin to see that life isn't something to shape. It's something to listen to, not with your ears, but with your presence. This is the kind of work that doesn't lead you anywhere. It meets you where you already are and then asks nothing of you but honesty."
-Perry "Dr. Octopus" Knoppert, founder, The Octopus Movement

"Laurie Seymour's book is a radiant gift—a sacred offering from someone who has walked the path of awakening and returned with treasures of truth. She writes about Source with rare authenticity, weaving her personal journey with universal wisdom."
-Nancy Swisher, MA, MFA, Transformational Coach, Spiritual Mentor, author of *The Life That Woke Me Up Was My Own: A Memoir*

"Laurie Seymour is what I call a Firefly—someone who shines her light brightly and generously shares it with the world. With the depth of a seasoned psychotherapist and the gift of intuitive knowing, she offers insights that are both profound and illuminating."
-Julie Wignall, Leadership Development, Strategy, and Community Creator, Award-winning author of *The Extraordinary Power of Fireflies*